BECKY
And Her Friends

ROLANDO
HINOJOSA

Arte Público P.
Houston
Texas
1990

This book is made possible by a grant from the National Endowment for the Arts, a federal agency.

Arte Público Press
University of Houston
Houston, Texas 77204-2090

Hinojosa, Rolando.
 Becky and her friends / Rolando Hinojosa.
 p. cm.
 ISBN 1-55885-006-6
 I. Title.
PS3558.I545B43 1990
813'.54–dc20   89-35418
                                                              CIP

Photo by Evangelina Vigil-Piñón

The paper used in this publication meets the minimum requirements of the American National Standard for Permanence of Paper for Printed Library Materials Z39.48-1984.

Klail City Death Trip Series
(In order of appearance)

Dedication

In particular, to everyone who has wished me ill luck. As you can see, it's brought nothing but more titles to the Series. This should probably teach you a lesson, but most likely it won't.

I also dedicate the novel to all those persons living or dead whose appearance here is merely coincidental.

And, to the friends, old and new, who've stayed by and with me, no matter what.

Finally, to two other Beckys, whom this one resembles not: Hurston's and Thackeray's. My thanks to them, too, of course.

Becky and Her Friends

The Opening Shot

What are we to do with Becky? What should we think of such a woman? A Texas Mexican who, apparently, from one day to the next, decides (that power-laden verb) that her husband is no longer going to live with her and with those two children of theirs?

And what of her mother, doña Elvira Navarrete, wife of Catarino Caldwell, Capt. U.S.A., Cav. Ret.? Yes, what will doña Elvira say? with her dreams of a long, lasting alliance with the Escobar-Leguizamón-Leyva families?

And what will the world say? The world that matters: Belken County, Klail City, the Valley. This world where people talk, and talk, and talk. And despite much of the foolishness which is said, sputtered out, and, at times, hissed out, the truth comes spilling out.

The listener is no P. Galindo, sad to say. P. Galindo knew people; the listener is a beginner.

The Valley, though old, is vigorous still. It has seen many rites, has produced many witnesses. In over 200 years of oral and recorded history, many generations have come and gone and taken their place in history in the cemeteries of the world: in this case, Europe, the Orient, wherever Valley men and women have died. Many lives and some miracles, but, as usual, more ordinary lives than miraculous ones.

All of this the listener knows, intuits even.

A brief prologue, then, and the listener is grateful to the Greeks for having invented the term. And, for this novel to begin, it'll start with another bit of Greek, a drama. In this case, a brief one.

And, since it is brief, the reader is warned that attention is an essential. The reader must be reminded, as if in wartime, that it isn't the firing or the shrapnel one worries about. One should worry more about the holes they leave on those who don't take care and cover. As always, verbum sat sapienti.

The novel begins here:

(A woman in her late thirties is standing. It's her living room; she picks up a candy wrapper and throws it a distance of some four feet and makes the basket. She smiles. While dressed nicely, she's not planning to leave the house. Not tense, not relaxed; nevertheless, she is quite sure of herself. She is waiting for someone; in this case, her husband. His name is Ira Escobar, a County Commissioner. A car's engine is heard and the closing of a door. He enters through a screened front porch and into the living room).

BECKY: "I ve decided that you are not going to live with us anymore."

IRA: "What?"

BECKY: (With indescribable patience.) "I've decided that you are not going to live with us anymore."

(Exit Ira Escobar, for now).

Becky Navarette → married to Ira Escobar

mother's brother

Geronimo Caldwell - father

mother is deceased

Cast of Characters
(in order of appearance)

Lionel Villa (Becky's uncle) *mother's side*
Viola Barragán – *married as correspondent of Independencia Becky's ci*
Isidro Peralta
Andrés Malacara
Emilio Tamez
Julia Ortegón *college friend*
Ursula Ortegón *Becky's Godmother*
Martín San Esteban
E. B. Cooke
Edith Timmens
Bowly Ponder
Lucas Barrón
Otila Macías Rosales
Reina Campoy
Bill and Tippy Ochoa
Gualberto Ornelas, O.M.I.
Sammie Jo Perkins
Polín Tapia
Noddy Perkins
Nora Salamanca
Matías Soto, O.M.I.
Elvira Navarrete
Raúl Santoscoy
Drinks González
Ira Escobar (county commissioner)
Becky

his partners

re married Julia Malacara

Well! some people talk of morality, and some
of religion, but give me a little snug property.

Maria Edgeworth

Lionel Villa

Let's drop in on Lionel Villa and hear what he has to say regarding Rebecca—alias Becky—Escobar. The famous Becky Escobar, wife for a certain time (in these uncertain times) of banker-politician cum horns, Ira Escobar, a native of Jonesville-on-the-Rio. This is the same Ira Escobar who graced Klail City (county seat of Belken County) and who now lives in Jonesville once again.

Now, you would think that Lionel Villa is hardly a reliable witness since he is Becky's uncle. Too, he has left her some land, some money, and much good will, but Villa is a stalwart. A bulwark his friends call him. He's a man of his word—hombre de palabra, and a man of respect, hombre de respeto. These two attributes have little to do with money in Villa's case. Because he's old, his upper seventies, the listener would guess, and because he's never broken his word or promise, he commands respect as who wouldn't? But enough of this preamble, let's listen to what he has to say.

Right! I myself baptized that girl over to San Francisco de Paula mission on the eastern edge of the Celeste Hermoso Ranch, the Navarrete land ... I, too, am a Navarrete, the maternal side, and so, Becky's mom and I are cousins germane, primos hermanos. She then married a Caldwell. Those are my bona fides, period.

Well now, it's no secret that my wife and I never had any kids, and that's why we decided, years ago, that whatever else happened, the land would stay in the family—en la familia, eh? And if it could be done, the money too would stay in the family, not the Church. I mean, our families built San Francisco Mission, and that's enough; probably more than enough to get some of us into God's heaven, right? So, with the Church business out of the way, the money, no matter how little it was, and the trust no matter how small it was, and the land, no matter how hard, dry, and poor it may have been, that too would stay in the family.

The listener takes a brief pause here. Lionel Villa lights up an unfiltered Camel. He then winks at me and says he's down to a pack a day. Incidentally, he says, the doctors he's consulted through the years are all dead. This, of course, is by the way.

Well, when we baptized Becky, we decided then and there that she'd be the one to get the land and all. No strings. No restrictions. Outright. And that was some thirty odd years ago, and the will is still in force, yessir.

As for Becky's mom, my cousin Elvira? Two words for her: tickled and pink.

The paperwork was all done by Romeo Hinojosa, the lawyer. He was fresh out of college back then, but he knew what he was doing, all right. Everything within this country's laws, and this country sure has got some laws, don't it? A great country, but you've got to watch those laws, leave you naked if you don't.

Well, according to that last will and testament of ours, Becky was to get a good part of the trust when she hit thirty-five. And she hit them flat out, but ... yeah, and let me point out that her divorce from Ira Escobar took place three months before she hit thirty-five and added to which, they'd had a 60-day cooling off period before that, and so let's not hear any wild talk about coincidences or anything like that. Now, if you don't take my word for it, I won't go on, won't say another word.

The truth. She divorced that jackass, but that was personal, between 'em.

Okay. Becky slams into her thirty-five years and the separation and divorce become part of history. All of this came pretty close like, but close don't count, and let me tell you this too: she—Becky, now—she didn't push the economic door on that jackass's face. Personally, I think she should have, but she didn't, and it was her money and her will to do with it what she wanted, and I have no say-so , period, period, period.

So here comes old Romeo Hinojosa, much older and much wiser, and he has some advice with him. Texas, he says, for all its damfool laws, still retains some Spanish laws regarding property —community property, see? So he, Hinojosa, he fixes it to where Becky's kids, Charlie and Sarah, are the benefactors. The heirs to the trust, see? And who's to care for the money till Charlie and Sarah come of age, when Charlie's twenty-seven and Sarah twenty-five?

The Bank. The Klail City First National with Jehu Malacara as the trust officer. As I said, I don't have a legal leg to stand on here, yo no tengo vela en este entierro, and I'm not about to get into that Becky— Jehu thing. None of my business anyways.

Now I'm going to shoot off some 180 degrees here. Talking about the late Javier Leguizamón—in the words of a famous Irishman: as fine a man as ever robbed the helpless. Now he too knew how to get the laws to serve him ... oh, yes. All proper. Sure. But to his benefit. Double sure.

So, when he up and dies—you and I both know that he and Angelita were childless ... well, he leaves a chunk, and that's a big chunk, to Ira Escobar. That's right, Becky's husband.

Once again Hinojosa steps in and then right back out. His advice to Becky was—not the way I'm saying it, but words to that effect—stay out. It's a mess. You've got enough to handle here. And he was right, but Romeo Hinojosa is Becky's attorney, and he added a wrinkle: He got Homer Torres, he represents Ira, see? He got Homer to add Charlie and Sarah to their father's will. Fair's fair, Romeo Hinojosa said. Becky agrees to stay out of it—free and clear, no consideration whatsoever— but the kids got to be protected by their father. Ha!

But I got to say this too. Ira did well by his kids, but as Romeo Hinojosa says: Put it on paper and let's have dates, proper signatures, and witnesses. I mean that's like looking at the traffic lights and at both sides of the street before you let the dog cross the street ahead of you. No need to take chances.

At first it looked like Becky got the short end of that stick and right away people—la gente, eh?—people said that Hinojosa'd been bought off. Couldn't resist a gift, a bribe, see? But they were wrong.

It was good advice, sound advice. Becky got to keep her money, my wife's and mine, see? There wasn't much, but what she got was all of it. And Charlie and Sarah got their father's share out of that community property.

Pretty Anglo-like, right? But that's okay. Took time for us to get used to their laws, but that's okay, too.

So that's where it stands. That land of my wife's and mine is out to Bascom. Hard by some Leguizamón holdings. And that's important 'cause Ira Escobar is a Leguizamón on his mother's side, and as I said, old Javier Leguizamón did leave that chunk to Ira, outright. Hm.

I know this don't come to much, not when you consider how much money this government has wasted away . . .

At this point Lionel Villa stops to rub his left knee. He points to it: with his chin. He says he broke his knee when he fell off a chinaberry tree. And, his father, old don Justo Villa, whipped him for it. A damfool thing Lionel says, smiling. Me falling, he says, and my father whipping me for it. (Laughing) never fell again, no sir.

But let's get a drink, and we'll talk some more.

Frosted drinks of cold limeade in hand, the listener and Lionel Villa take a seat, on the ground, facing a cedar windbreak. The Rio Grande at their backs and less than a quarter mile away as it meanders its way toward the Gulf.

It's late September. The cotton's gone now, the third and lean pick was done with ten days ago. What few stubborn stalks of cotton remain have been turned black to gray by the Valley's own soil.

As I was saying just now, my cousin Elvira Navarrete was tickled and pink with the terms of the divorce. Not happy, with, the divorce, though, since that meant that Becky, now no longer an Escobar, could not then lay claim to the name Leguizamón. Elvira is like that, poor thing. Still, time and money have a way with smoothing things out, making things come out even.

And Becky, you ask? Oh, Becky . . . Ah, Becky. She had finally got rid of that anchor, and talk about turning over new leaves here and there. First it was Spanish. She was going to learn it again after years of nothing but English. Back to grade one, you might say, and good for her, say I.

And funny? Like a kid, see? She'd say some things in Spanish that would make you laugh or cry. Ha! But mistakes or not, she'd keep at it. Sounded like those Jewish merchants in Jonesville's Gaza Strip, mixing the languages, not giving up ... And Becky won out. It was a lack of practice, but it came back.

But the best part was about the clubs in Klail. She quit 'em. The women's, the music. That kind of shit.

And speaking of shit, while the money and the land and the kids was agreed to, Ira Escobar—on his own—well, he tried to muddy it up a bit.

How—he'd ask—how could anyone say that Becky was a good mother when everyone knew she'd tied herself to a certain someone or other. Well, that was a pile of bull.

Becky did find someone, Jehu Malacara, the banker. But tied? Living with? Arrimados? No sir. Married, and in Dellis County. That's legal, isn't it? I admit Dellis is a no-count county, but it's still part of the State of Texas, ain't it?

And Jehu's a good man. I've seen him with the kids—and I see how they look to him, too. Jehu's no saint, he never said or lay claim to, and he didn't pretend to be one either in any way. He's a good man. Jehu's got a pair on him that clang when he walks. Serious, decent.

All right, take a look at this: at the Bank there, who's in charge? Noddy Perkins? Gettin' old and tough enough still, but he could hardly wait for Jehu to get back from Austin some years back. He—Noddy—he knew Jehu'd be back at the Bank. One, two, three years, was it? And Jehu did come back. Took his time getting back, but when he did, the job was still waiting for him.

And you know what Ira Escobar said back then? And he said it here, in that house where you got that drink. Said it was luck that Jehu got the job back. Luck, he said. That boy could no more read character than I could sing in the opera house. Hmph! Luck! This, he said. That, he said. Ira es poca cosa, that's right. No count.

Jehu came in through the front door of Perkins's bank. In he comes, someone tells Noddy, and out comes that old pirate, and shakes Jehu's hand like he was priming a kerosene pump.

I can imagine how Ira must've taken this. Yeah, Ira the commissioner of Place Four. But there was nothing he could do about it—so he lied to himself by calling it luck. You've got to feel sorry for a person like that. He—Ira—owed his job to Noddy and to that uncle of his, Javier Leguizamón. But he doesn't have power—el poder—ha! Money? Sure. Land? I'll go along with that. But power? No, not a bit of it.

Hate to say it, but I got to: I've always said he doesn't have what it takes to give bad news to someone or to accept the good news when it comes. He calls it luck.

But Jehu? A different story all together; he can be tough, but he knows how to be soft, tender, even. Knows how to laugh, too. And don't no one come by this farm to tell me that Jehu had it easy as a child, boy, or youngster. He didn't.

He's not Noddy's fool, and I've yet to see Jehu back down from what's right.

Remember the time with him and Martín San Esteban, the pharmacist? Olivia's brother?

And remember Olivia? Bright girl, and good. Made for Jehu. Steady. And then to die in a car wreck? Some damn drunk ... And Jehu? At the hospital, ten days, two weeks, whatever. From there to Witwer's Mortuary and from there to holy ground.

They'd been engaged, and formally. Un noviazgo, like the old days. You were there, remember? And you think Moisés San Esteban and his wife would have approved of that engagement if Jehu wasn't a serious person? That they were going to consent their one daughter, Livita, to someone without any sense? No, not by a long chalk.

Jehu, like his dad or maybe his grandfather before him, went for Livita San Esteban's hand—alone. No sponsors, nothing. Borrowed his cousin Rafe's car and drove to the San Esteban home. Like the old days, back when I was a kid. Two requests, the engagement and the right to visit, to call on her there. At home. You don't see that anymore. But he did it. And he went alone when he did.

An hour later? Back in the car and Jehu drove straight to the pharmacy. That's right, to see Martín San Esteban, his brother-in-law to be. Martín's got some Becerra blood to go along with the San Esteban mixture, and he can be dense at times. Bull headed, even.

Martín started to fuss while Jehu crossed his arms and stood there, legs apart. Just then Martín's own wife rushed in and told—that's told—told Martín not to be such a damned fool. I think that's the first time Martín San Esteban got wind who it was he'd married when he married San Juanita, old Pedro Ycaza's only daughter. This is not to say that Jehu needed help, 'cause he didn't.

San Juanita Ycaza knew what kind of person Jehu Malacara was—just like good cotton, a long staple and none of that middling stuff.

And I know this happened for a fact, and I know it as many others in Klail know it. I mean, how big is Klail anyway? Yeah.

Well, then what happened, happened. Some drunk Anglo came barrelin' off the old Military Highway, fails to make that curve, and he hits Olivia broadside. And just how long had she and Jehu been engaged? Seven, eight months? Something like that? In a wreck. Three blocks from her house. Son-of-a-bitch.

And then some six months go by. By now, Ira Escobar—damned fool—decides on his own to run for County Judge. Doesn't bother to ask the Bank, doesn't bother to check with Noddy Perkins ... Well, you got to admire guts like that, but that's a very limited boy.

Now, I've got nothing against being independent, but when you go on your own after you gave your heart and your soul to someone, like Ira did, what does he expect?

The mexicanos weren't going to vote for him—he's Noddy's boy. On the other hand, they got nothing against Jehu, he works there. That's different.

County Judge. Hmph. About this time I wind up in the hospital, and things are looking bad—bad to the point where I'm going to be calling Death on a first name basis. The heart, they said. No, it's the liver, they said. Your mother! is what I said. Four doctors ... Jesus!

So who comes to see me at the hospital, aside from family? I'll tell you. Jehu. Yeah. To talk, that's all. To laugh some. I got, I got some forty years on that boy. And he didn't come to see me on business and not 'cause we're related, which we're not. A visit. To talk.

I tell you, it's a dirty shame but damn few of Jehu's generation know what manners are all about. And my boy Ira? Sure, he was there, but because Becky came to see me and it was there as God and the forty thousand virgins are my witnesses, it was right there that I knew that Becky would be off and flying, flying away like a dove. That girl was going to leave, and if I was going to die, why, it was time for the lawyer Hinojosa to go over all my papers. One more time. Which he did.

But like I said, Becky was just too much woman for Ira Escobar. And if they lasted as long as they did—I mean, if she put up with that jackass as long as she did, it was due to that eternal stupidity, that so-called tradition. And here's another truth: Becky's mother, yes, my cousin Elvira Navarrete, kept that marriage going. Ha!

Mother, hmph. Giving birth doesn't make a woman a mother. No sir. And she's my cousin, no two ways about that. Ira—she'd say—Ira is a Leguizamón, and she'd puff up like a blow fish. A lot of that wedding and marriage was her doing. And Becky married him.

Good Lord. And of course, since it was to be the wedding of the last two centuries, they went all out. And here's poor Catarino Caldwell—the father of the bride—and who is just about nutty enough to build a new church, see what I mean? Old Catarino has always had more cents than sense, more property than brain cells. Where's my proof? Well, look who he married, my cousin!

That Becky has a spine on her, though, and a brain to go with it, and more of both than her parents, and that's not a matter of luck. I'll be the first to say that her mother can be a loose cannon at times, but she's not a

Becky's mother

bad person, you know what I mean? She's not cruel or mean, just dumb
and as tiresome as a summer drought ... And Catarino? Not a mean
bone there either, I'll tell you. Now you hand him a rifle, a fishing rod,
and he's off, hunting, fishing, trapping. Catarino Caldwell made himself
into a mexicano years ago, even before the time Becky was born. Tell
you what, I bet there's not a hundred people left in the Valley, farm or
city folks, who've heard him say a word in English. God's truth. Just like
Martín Holland, he's La Güera Fira's daddy. Yeah. You remember her,
she's that good looking blondie married up with Elías Castro. Those
two, Martín and Catarino Caldwell Mexicanized themselves early.

But I was saying, Becky is neither dumb nor bad looking. That she
married Ira Escobar is something else again. Her mom pushed and
shoved mountains—it was scandalous—and Becky, dutiful, young, in-
experienced, gave in. She'd had four years at college and the diploma
to go with them and then to end up married to that jackass. Damn!

But we all've got just one life to live and lead, and if you play your
cards poorly, if you fold too soon, life and happiness—all the pleasures,
yeah, and the suffering too—fly out the window. And life goes out dull
as mud, too.

But then that's why friends and relatives were invented, and that's
where I came in, had to.

Becky had to become independent. Economically independent, you
get me? And someone else came in too: a woman, a woman with nerve
and fiber, unafraid, and gutsy. And sharp, too.

The listener and Lionel Villa walked back to the farm house for
some ice, for some more limeade, and for another pack of Camel cigarettes. Lionel Villa looked up at the Gulf-laden clouds and bet the listener, giving odds of four to seven, that there'd be no rain that day. The
listener, with a farmer for a father, didn't take the bet. The wind was
coming in from the South, the listener said. Villa's laugh cackled somewhat and this brought out a couple of dogs resting under the house.
Would I bet that the Gulf hurricane would miss the Valley, he asked.
The listener is much younger than Lionel Villa, but no fool.

On the way back to the windbreak, Villa said the woman he was
talking about was the redoubtable Viola Barragán.

So Viola stepped in to help Becky, help her with a little boost, to make her independent. Her own person. Ha! And then, my cousin Elvira ... did I tell you?

Ha! Not a peep out of her. Yeah. Now, way back there, when I was young—younger—around the twenties, the nineteen thirties, Viola and Elvira were a pair of good-looking beauties. Train stoppers, you know what I am talking about? Just plain, uncommon beauty, the both of them. You've got to admit that Becky is a looker, and she'll be a looker at fifty, even. Well, her mom, my cousin Elvira, didn't take a back seat to anyone—prettier than anyone of those Hollywood actresses. Oh, yeah. She'll keep, all right. You won't find any rust on Elvira and let me tell you that Viola ran just about even. Neck to neck, no daylight, just like the horse-racing, let me tell you.

And both married young, just like Becky, but younger. Becky had the college and all, but marrying young just like that domineering mama of hers. 'Cause let me tell you this too: Elvira Navarrete is no weakling; she's unafraid. But she's got a weakness, she's a climber. And that is exactly where she pushed Becky, nose first and come what may. And there Elvira went, pushing, shoving her Becky to the Leguizamón clan.

Why, a blindman can see how dumb Ira Escobar is. You won't find him hiding his light under no bushel basket. First, there's no light, and second, there's no basket either. No idea how to hold one ... But I got to admit, limited as that boy is, he and Becky made one fine-looking couple. What they didn't make was a marriage. Simple as that. But I also got to admit that Becky worked like a slave for some ten years there so Ira'd be and stay on as a county commissioner. I now think that it was right there and right then that she saw what it was she'd married. Probably saw it before, sensed it maybe, felt it, somehow, but she wasn't the person to judge her husband. She just flat, straight out had not thought on it.

And so she married. She dressed well, ate at the best places that Klail City and the Valley have to offer. But no fool, Becky saw right away that Ira was successful in politics because of the Klail-Blanchard-Cooke Ranch. And the Bank, of course, they all being the same thing. She wised up.

So she flitted here'n there, like a butterfly. But she lived for him, not for her. She was a messenger. A flunky, for God's sake. And she lived for her mother. God!

And Elvira, her mom? Happier than a dozen clams, I'm here to tell you. And Becky again? Politicking for her husband. And what was she doing for herself, for Becky Escobar? Nothing. Not a thing.

Shoot. The Ranch and the Bank did the important things that truly mattered. Becky was a prop, visible here and there, but a prop. She was

being used just like Sammie Jo Perkins who ... hold it! Sorry. I'm on
shaky ground here, but I might as well say what I think I know:

Sammie Jo's father, Noddy Perkins, used his only daughter, Sammie Jo, as a brood mare. Yes ... Noddy married her off to a couple of
absolute—total—no count losers. Talk was one of them was a fancy boy,
or both of them was ... It doesn't matter. Noddy saw his own daughter
the same way he saw Becky Escobar: a tool, something to use.

I wasn't fooled a bit back then. Not for one minute, I wasn't. It was
Noddy's idea and no one else's that Becky Escobar be given unanimous
membership in those clubs I mentioned earlier this morning. Noddy.
His idea, no one else's. And Becky? Blind, blinded by all that dazzle,
by all that attention. Poor thing.

And she told me so, herself. Told me the day she first thought of
a divorce. That's another story altogether, and a long one, too. But I
heard it from her. And I don't blame anyone, and I won't point fingers
at anyone. Not Sammie Jo, either. No one. If anything, she and Becky
became good friends after the divorce.

At this point, Lionel Villa invited the listener for another light snack.
Nothing special, he said. He brewed some tea, orange-leaf tea, and
each of us used a cinammon stick as a stirring spoon. Both Villa and
the listener sucked the stick dry and popped it into the orange-leaf tea.

Did I mention the Spanish, I mean when she decided to use it again?
Well, when she talked to me of her life as a flunky, she referred to herself
as a pendeja, a fool, an asshole, really. Not angry, more of a realization,
of a wasted part of her life—but I will say this as clearly as I can: Becky
acted on her own. She reached and made a firm decision, and she didn't
ask her mother either, no sir. Becky was going to cut loose from Ira, and
she was cutting that umbilical cord from Elvira too, see?

A decision firm and personal. No crying, no hiccups, no shortness
of breath, and no raising of the voice. In short, class! She told Ira that
they weren't going to live together anymore. That's all she said to that
jackass: that they would not be living together anymore, and that that

was it.

But the people? What would they say? And the families? And society, too? Friends? And X, and Y, and Z, and every damned busybody to boot, including their bloody mother? Nothing to do with me is what that great beauty said. This is of no concern, of no business, really, to the family, the families, Klail's society, etc. It's no one's business. No one's. And Becky went on, since it doesn't matter to me—and she told me this, all smiles when she told me .... You seen that smile of hers?

Anyway, she said: "If it doesn't matter to me, whatever the world thinks or wants to think, is of no concern either." So, Klail, the world, everyone, could take a flying leap at the moon, the nearest lake, the Rio Grande ...

But that was it. That union was over, and that was that.

Becky herself called Chalo Figueroa from Valley Movers, and she packed everything that belonged to Ira. Everything and by herself, too. All this according to Chalo Figueroa. And she paid for the move, too, although the lawyer Hinojosa did recover part of the expenses later on when it came to divving up the community property.

Oh, and another thing. She got some additional money, yeah. All those years they were married and that Ira worked at the Klail Bank, and he was under a generous retirement plan? Well, she got part of that, too. For the kids, Becky said.

And she didn't do that from spite. The house and another share of the property that was coming to her, and that was it. And then, to have a friend in Viola Barragán, that was a bonus. As I said, Viola and Becky's mom had been—have been—close for years.

Anyone who's met Viola knows she's not a pushover, and if sometime back she saw Becky as willful and foolish, everyone now also admits that it was Viola—first and before anyone else—who recognized that Becky's talents had been hidden for years.

Too, that Becky, in her foolish stage, used to think that Viola Barragán was a nobody, an over-the-hill man chaser, something like that, a devil in a skirt, as we say. Anyway, Becky also saw for herself that having to depend on someone else for a living, to depend on someone else for anything, to be nothing but a kept-though-married-woman was not the way to live. She saw what being independent meant.

And they hit it off. Right away.

Viola has always been a believer of allowing people to do, to live, as they want. There are some who say Viola goes overboard on this, but what do people know, right? Now, what Viola Barragán does have is a pair of ovaries that would serve as testicles on a prize Santa Gertrudis bull. Viola doesn't go around begging, asking favors, etcetera. She's got a keen eye, and the world is just going to have to deal with that. She's no gossip, either. No intriguer, she doesn't go around making life hard for anyone. And she's forgiving. How 'bout that?

She'll forgive—perhaps not forget, but she's firm in compassion, I'll say that. If Viola, sometime back, said that Becky Escobar was a ninny, let's say, Viola had every right to say what she pleased, just like everybody else. And she may have been right on the money 'cause Becky was allowing herself to be used. Becky was blinder than a family of bats. She couldn't even see the tip of her own little upturned nose. She used someone else's eyes to see through, like wearing blinders.

But when she took the blinders off, threw away that blindman's cane, that's when she took a deep, deep breath and in that breath she sent Ira off, up, and away. But it didn't stop there, with her husband. Out too went those secondhand ideas and opinions she used to hang on to.

It was the change, see? A new woman, really, and that's why her mamma Elvira didn't know what to do, what to think. Whoever that woman was, it wasn't Becky, thought Elvira—who almost fainted. No. No. No. It's a devil, a ghost of some kind ... Elvira all over.

Well, just as soon as Viola got wind of Becky's doings, Viola drove from Klail to Jonesville to see Elvira. To head her off, really. And then—just as soon as she got to Elvira's house—Viola took her aside and spoke in no uncertain, unreserved terms. Not to act the damned fool, for one. That she—Elvira—better not think, better not even think, of saying anything harsh to Becky. That Becky in her present state and sailing high, that Becky with two kids and with thirty-five years on her back, that Becky in that mood of hers now, would and could tell Elvira—mother or not—to leave her nose out of Becky's affairs. To stick to her own business, if she—Elvira—had any. And so on.

And Viola it was who could make Elvira see the light. She and Elvira, remember? Well, they've been friends through and through and friendship, after all, must stand for something; I mean, what's friendship for if one can't tell certain truths in no uncertain terms?

And my cousin didn't butt in, held her peace, and for this Becky was grateful.

Later, much later, when Becky and Viola joined up, Becky learned that it'd been Viola Barragán who had held Elvira in check. And because of that ... well, it's because of Viola that mother and daughter get on so well. Although, truth in place, Elvira looks at Becky with a bit of fear mixed with pride, somehow, because she—Becky—had the nerve to shed, be rid of, Ira Escobar as a worn out, cracked piece of luggage.

You live long enough, as the saying goes, right? And now? Becky is as enterprising as Viola. As for her life with Jehu Malacara, that's their life. They're both over twenty-one. People will talk, though, and even now, married and all, people in Klail City are still going to talk, criticize, whatnot . . . .

If Becky has one remorse it may be that she didn't jettison Ira much sooner, but that's like week-old bread, you may as well throw as much water on it as possible. Same thing, water and distance between them, oh yes. Life's shorter than a quarter-horse race and you can't afford to look back, and so on, and so forth. I'm telling you, Becky cut that growth away, and the cutting was the onliest thing that mattered, you with me?

Look, why don't we just cross the River two miles down from here, and you, my wife, and I will eat some honest-to-goodness food.

Lionel Villa is Becky's uncle who set up an inheritance for her when turned 35. Supportive of Becky + talks against Ira.

Viola Barragán

Lionel Villa is now followed by Viola Barragán: businesswoman, world traveler and resident of Mexico, India, South Africa, the German Federal Republic, (in that order), three times a widow (Agustín Peñalosa, M.D., Karl-Heinz Schuler, Harmon Gillette), and friend-mentor-protector of Jehu Malacara, Vice President and newly-appointed Cashier at the Klail City First National Bank. Viola is called that, Viola, by her friends.

She's doña to everyone else, and that includes the listener.

Yes, it's a bit thick and bothersome too, to be called doña, but I can't deny I'm 59-years-old, and the full-length mirror is always there to remind me of it in case I forget.

That stupid bromide about the alternative to growing old is as dry as yesterday's news. But there's nothing one can do about it, age and death are the two immutables ....

But to the point. I've known Becky from day one; I was there at Jonesville's Mercy Hospital the day she was born. And her dad? My compadre Catarino Caldwell? Why, I've known him since he was stationed at Fort Jones, a cavalryman. This takes us back to 1938, maybe '37. By that time, well, by then—see?—me and Elvira Navarrete were friends, close friends. Closer than close. We were tight, and still are.

Fact too is that we gave people plenty to talk about in those days, and that's the truth, pure, unlacquered, and unvarnished.

Elvira and I, we liked guys and made no bones about it. It's a natural fact. Of course, there wasn't much of an opportunity to go out with them, but where there's a will, right? And we'd sneak out once in a

26

while, not often enough, though.

Elvira's folks owned two cars in those days; *gente de posibles*, see? Monied. And I knew back then, and I was in my early teens, that Elvira's father, old don Julio Navarrete, aside from owning a pharmacy, also owned two gaming houses, plus a couple of dance-cantinas where the men paid to dance. Here I'm talking about El Farolito and La Golondrina. Old don Julio owned some land, too. City lots. So, the Navarretes had money in the thirties, during the Depression. And he was also a first-class hypocrite, and like most hypocrites, he liked to brag on himself. To me, bragging's a weakness of character. Like an embryo which is half-finished, not fully developed. You know exactly what I mean.

One example ought to do it, but it needs backgrounding. No sense saying otherwise; my parents married me off to Agustín Peñalosa when I was going on sixteen. Agu was a Northerner, un norteño, from Agualeguas, Nuevo León. A north borderman, then. He was closing in on thirty-three about that time, and he was all set as a medical surgeon and all. Spoke some English, too.

In a word, he spoiled me. As for bedtime, he was steady and regular—and I never, not once, betrayed him, his trust, his confidence, or his bed. Sounds funny, self-serving even now, forty-two years later, but I didn't even think of another man. He was mine, and I was his. Simple as that.

The future? It looked and promised everything I wanted. Oh, I was a bit of a lump and foolish, but you have to remember I was a kid. Dumb and all the rest that goes with it. Life was rosy. I felt safe. Cared for.

My folks, now, they weren't out begging in the streets, either. But my dad, he was a visionary, always helping people out. That he received little or no thanks and no gratitude was of no concern to him. And he didn't preach, no sir. No sermonizing. He loved me and he loved my mother. And confidence? In me? To the fullest. And he was patience itself. Now, right now, at my age, I see that what he did should be called love. The late P. Galindo was way ahead of everyone on that score. He knew what my father was: gente decente, a good man.

But where was I? Oh—I was talking about old don Julio Navarrete … Well, when Agustín died that stupid death of his, I moved out of our house and went to stay with my folks again.

Rafe Buenrostro's dad, El Quieto, he took charge of the estate. For one, he got a good price for the house Agustín had had built for me. Don Jesús El Quieto also straightened out the Mexican bank accounts, some bonds, and he placed the money at the Klail City Savings and at the Bank; shares, not savings, eh? It was a right fair account, and El Quieto sat me down and showed me how to get things done. For and by myself, he always said.

Around this time, Noddy Perkins was about twenty-something years old and learning whatever there is to learn about the banking business. And it was Noddy who took time to show me what real estate meant. What it could do, more importantly, what it couldn't do. And we went to bed ... oftener than with Agustín, but Noddy's always had a limited imagination when it comes to sex.

Well, Don Jesús El Quieto, as executor, arranged for the sale of the house, tightened up the bank accounts and invested. Conservative but safe; banks were failing all over the place. My folks? Happy and contented, and guess what I did then—I must've been nineteen then—well, I took on old Javier Leguizamón as a lover. Well, that didn't last. Didn't amount to much either, and the man was a miser ... but what stopped that affair was something my mother said in passing. She had no idea, of course. And then again, maybe she did. Something to be said about not preaching and screaming...

My mom was a friend to doña Angelita, Javier's wife, and that did it for me.

Nothing doing is what I said. Fair's fair. That's how the game is played or not at all. Luckily for me, about this time Gela Maldonado came on stage, made her debut. And she didn't have to either. She liked la vida—the life. Javier Leguizamón wanted both of us, a real macho, see? But I was all set for retirement. And Gela? She was all for it. She liked the idea of three in a bed. Well, in this case, three's a crowd is not just a cliché.

I like the bed, and if I like the guy, let's go and no holds barred. I've loved, been loved, here and abroad. But there is something I won't put up with, and that's sharing the bed. I like what's mine to be mine, so, when Gela jumped into the picture it was " ... so long, Javier," for me.

And I was ready to leave him, anyway, and what he proposed is something I just don't agree with ... I'm not talking about hypocrisy or about me being a goody-goody. Goes beyond that, but it doesn't matter, and not now at any rate. So we broke.

And so the sun set only to rise again. It couldn't have been more than a month later when old don Julio Navarrete—Elvira's dad ... and he was around Javier Leguizamón's age more or less—don Julio came up and blew something in my ear. As it were.

To me! His daughter's best friend! That type of thing. Happens much too much, but here I was a kid, and I got scared. That's a dangerous man, that type of person. He went after me, and then, are you ready? He went after his own daughter. Why, that's just plain monstrous. Why even thinking about it is just as bad. Isn't it?

Well, I told him to go to Hell and stay there. Straight out. I kept seeing Elvira, and though I didn't much want to, I went in and out of

the house just like always. And then Elvira told me. One of the sad-
dest days of this life of mine. Well, after that, we were always together.
Protection, see?

And, too, I couldn't stop going to her house, how would that have
looked?

But I would never stay alone in the same room with that man, and I
never did. We never did.

A brief recess. The listener, relaxed, is sitting in V.B.'s office on what
must be one of the longest sofas in the Free World. Brocade, too.

Viola Barragán had raised her hand, thus putting a stop to her story.
Sitting behind the glass-topped desk, almost as large as the sofa, she
pressed a button set in a plastic box full of lights and buttons.

A phone, one she doesn't have to pick up or cradle. It's business,
and she calls people in her four-story office building. The conversations
are short, but not cold, and the orders precise, exact. The gold-tipped
Parker fountain pen is for figures, not for doodling.

An incoming call, the only one was from Becky herself. To hear her
voice is to see her: attractive, bright, and the listener, who knows Becky,
although not well, can tell she smiles as she talks. The listener knows
many people who've tried to smile and talk at the same time. He also
knows it's hard to do. Actors do it all the time, the listener knows, but
it's their job; their profession calls for it.

But Becky is no actress.

And here's doña Viola Barragán again.

We're up to 1939. The Spring of. And it's rained a lot here and there
since that time.

It was a bit breezy that April in the Valley. A late Easter, too. And
I remember sitting at home, alone, and bored, when I left the sofa,
headed for the bathroom, showered, fixed myself up and decided to go
to Jonesville. Alone and by bus. But don't ask me why. It happened.

I say this because I've tried to remember why it was I wanted to go
to Jonesville. I mean, why not Ruffing, going north not east, or why not
Bascom, to the west? And why a bus? Of all things. Oh, sure, Elvira

lived and lives in Jonesville, but I'm sure I wasn't going to see her. I would've telephoned first, see? I just did it, and I can't remember why I did so.

What happened after that is common knowledge, not to say notorious: I met up with Karl-Heinz, and I fell like a rock. I was giddy, really. And he loved me! Thanks be to God and the changes He brings . . . .

married

My folks? Transfixed, hypnotized, and happy for the both of us. And there was Karl-Heinz and his carroty hair, eyes like blue crystal, and speaking Spanish like a gachupín, a Spaniard right off the boat. In my case, Peninsular Spanish has always made me laugh, by the way.

And if I cried for Agustín, and I did—I'm not made of iron—I cried even more for my German. A good, clear-cut diamond of the first water, that Karl-Heinz Schuler. Gente decente. At any other time in history— except this one—he would've had a brilliant career. He knew diplomacy and tact and discretion. Name it.

We suffered together and we had great, marvelous times together; and I guess that's why I still miss him so, and it's been over twenty years, now. Things, that's what we did. Things . . .

And speaking of things, this brings me right back to old don Julio Navarrete, Elvira's dad, Becky's grandfather . . . As I'd said, aside from the pharmacy and the gaming houses, and the cantina dancing houses— which most people knew nothing about—he also owned a whorehouse. Here in Klail, over by the Grand Canal. Probably Klail's only whore- house. Later, a big one, in Flora . . . .

Well, at that time, Fira Holland entered the life. Her dad, old Martín Holland, had married a mexicana, a poor one. And Martín, although an enlisted man, was good friends with Catarino Caldwell, Becky's dad. A few years back, Estéfana Holland, maybe her name was Epifania— anyway, the Holland woman died, and left Martín a widower with little Fira. Get this: the Hollands were legally married, Church and state. So she dies, and little Fira's about eleven-years-old at this time. Twelve, top.

Martín begins to drink and Fira, a natural-born beauty if there is such a thing, was taken in by the González family. Uncles and aunts and all of them crazier than loons on or off the ground. I mean crazy- mad-insane: the men preached and the women dressed like nuns. And they sang, too. Aleluyas, rollers, is what they were.

You can imagine Fira's shame—and at that age: out on the street with them, that gaggle of silly geese. Embarrassing. No, not embarrass- ing, unbearable. Poor little girl. At age sixteen she left Jonesville and only looked back to check that she wasn't being followed.

So, out of Jonesville, and now she's got to eat, so she became a waitress 'cause that's where the food is. From waitressing to dancing in Navarrete's cantina, and from dancing to whoring: one-two-three.

After that? A life like a bad Mexican movie. My folks thought they'd
seen her here in Klail around that time, perhaps a bit after. During
World War II. Me? I was in India or in South Africa, it was a concentration camp, the South Africans invented them or the English .... So,
I lost track of poor Firita Holland.

But the stars remain in place, don't they? Doesn't matter what we
say or do. Anyway, a few years later, I ran into P. Galindo; on his last
legs and days about that time. Dying as we spoke, he was.

Anyway, Galindo told me—and I now see him clear as anything,
because he had a drink with me. He wasn't supposed to, but "It doesn't
matter anymore," he said at the time. Anyhow, it seems that way back
there, when Fira was a starving kid—years and years ago—that Fira ran
out of Klail and fast. And scared, Galindo said. Navarrete had wanted
to put her in a house—oh, she was whoring all right, but free lancing.
An independent, and that way she could pick and choose. For pay, of
course, and what else could she do? She had to eat. But she took care of
herself. I'm not talking about rich guys here, I'm talking about hygiene.

But old man Navarrete meant to corral her. Control her, and the
fear he put in her was the size of a Baldwin Grand Piano. Stuck in a
whorehouse, worse than prison.

And I found out through Galindo and as reliable a person as there
is, or was, in his case. How reliable? He drove Fira back to Jonesville.
Yes, he did, in that little Ford he owned back then. Had a rumble seat,
and maroon-colored ... you ever see it?

So, Galindo drove Fira Holland to Jonesville and checked her into
a hotel, a good one. The Belken Gardens itself, I think it was. That was
a long time ago ... and Fira eventually got married and now she's been
married for years to one of the River Road Castros ... the red heads.

Old Galindo. He was more faithful to his Paulita than he ever could
be to his country, flag, or religion. And discreet? Took many a secret,
many a confidence with him. Galindo knew a lot of the world and its
ways ... And I bet he never left the Valley to do so, only the once, when
the U.S. Army came and took neighborhoods full of mexicanos. He
knew the world by heart. Nothing surprised Galindo. And yet, he wasn't
a cynic.

Galindo was one of the Chosen, and he'd been chosen to carry Fira
across the desert and into Jonesville's Promised Land. He was there,
available. A man whose discretion was longer than the Rio Grande.
One of the Chosen ....

It was only when he was about to die that he told me of the trip to
Jonesville, of old don Julio Navarrete's filth. Yeah, don Julio Navarrete,
a whole man they called him at the funeral. A whore man was more like

it, and that's what Galindo called him. Padrote, padrotón ...

A son-of-a-bitch, and a bully add up to a coward, and that's what Julio Navarrete was.

Elvira never spoke of her father to me again. That was our secret. Never again, not a word, and you've got to remember that Elvira and I go back years and years ... Oh, yes.

And a good part of that friendship is why I like Becky. And not to criticize here, but to me, they, Elvira and Catarino, raised her as a bolillita, an Anglo girl. Big mistake! I mean, a big mistake on Elvira's and Catarino's part. Why, the Texas Anglos looked at them, the Caldwells, as Mexicans, at least here in Klail City they did. Poor th ... but what am I saying? Poor nothing, Becky was her own person from the start. She just hadn't found her own way. But she did, I'll say.

Lunch on Viola. She spoke into that plastic box of hers and ordered some take out: "Catfish all right with you?" she asked. "Iced tea? No dessert? You sure?"

And that was that for now. She went over some figures from several sets of books and would talk to someone or someones on the box—she just talked into it and this left both hands free to work on something else at the same time.

The rectangular shaped office measured some ten by twenty maybe more. Cream-colored; the color said nothing about the person. The usual certificates and obligatory photographs with local and state politicians. A letter from the President of the United States, but who'd signed it was anybody's guess.

On one corner an IBM-PC gathering dust on its cover. The rug was best eight-ply, easily. One could see that. The rug, too, said nothing about its owner.

The listener decided this was an indifferent office, meant to say nothing, designed to reveal nothing: the wall safes were plainly visible, nothing to hide here.

And that was it, its owner told you point blank: nothing to hide here, no need to.

But, of course, all of us have something to hide ....

Sharp as a needle describes Becky, nothing less. A double-edged needle is Becky, and she's made of strong fiber, too. In and out, what you see in Becky is what you'll get.

She'd been here working for me for about six months, and in that time she knew all of the help inside out. Read the suppliers and merchandisers, too. And she knew how to work, how to set an example. The first thing she sloughed off was that reticence of hers, it smacked of snobbism, somehow. But she overcame that, and she was defining herself, learning about herself, knowing just who the hell she was, and that's always a big job. Too big for some.

So ... since she's finer than a stick pin, she began to study the business. And I came out ahead there; no question. Becky knew. She could see things, and I knew she knew. She's talented, I'm telling you. And hungry, and that always helps.

And there she is: what I can't cover, she does, and she does it and adds to it. That spells success, nothing less.

Let's go back to last summer. It had been a so-so year, profits, sure, but not much growth, so I took off for two months. I'd never done that before. A vacation, the very first one in my life, since the death of my Karl-Heinz!

Since the fifties, it had been work-work-work, but Becky changed all of that for me. Yes, she did . . . .

As for Elvira, she doesn't know a thing about anything. Why, even now, when Elvira and I get together, she'll mewl and pule some—the divorce, for Christ's sake! God in heaven knows that may be going on three years now. Oh, it's nothing to do with Catholicism or the Church. No!

Look here, the Valley's Mexican Catholic Church wears some pretty loose sleeves and garments, when it suits her to do so. Garments that would cover a multitude, know what I mean?

Does it take my money for donations here and there? Bet on it. It takes it, and I get my thanks, day and night, in rain or shine. And if the Church needs excuses to do so, all it's got to do is to look it up in some Bible or other, in some dogma, tenet. Name it. And . . .

Okay, this takes me to the late, lamented Father Pedro Zamudio— and that hook nose of his and as bald as the Americans' eagle. Don Pedro Zamudio came to the Valley as a babe in arms, same as I did. My folks carried me in from Mexico and don Pedro came in through the port at Jonesville with his Spanish parents. And landed here with those crazy gachupín ideas, that ridiculously insolent Spanish su-pe-ri-o-ri-ty, la superioridad española. Jesus ... No matter that they came here starving to death and all they owned was one hand in front and one in back when they walked. They had two other kids, all boys, and don Pedro was the Benjamín, the baby.

So what became of the Zamudio family? The two oldest boys became Valley mexicanos, Mexicans, but from this side of the Rio. And their parents? Don Tomás and doña Cleotilde? They soon lost that lisping sound of theirs; it's almost insulting the way it's thrown at you. Dropped it—the ceceo, they call it. And they settled into good people. No better than anyone else, no worse either. They were human beings, after all, and adiós my superiority.

And a good thing, too: they weren't Spaniards anymore. Not in Texas, in the Valley. They, the Zamudios, beat us here by twenty years, and they had to make certain adjustments, just like everybody else.

Do you—just by chance—do you happen to know that gachupín uncle of Rafe Buenrostro's? He thought, the uncle did, that he was something special. He then married into the Buenrostro family, and he soon got rid of those ideas. The Buenrostros are a serious lot; they won't put up with any stuff, no sir.

I'm saying all of this because of the Navarrete family. They were old Mexicans, mexicanos viejos, but at one time they thought of themselves as Spaniards; can you beat that? Just like the Leguizamóns. Oh, sure. The Leguizamóns considered themselves Spaniards for a while there. They're a bunch of obliging shits, they are. And they're the first to spot which way the wind is blowing, too.

And get this: they'd been mexicanos on another occasion, and then they became Spaniards. How 'bout that? Talk about your turncoats!

And Becky too had similar bents, similar pretensions in that pretty head of hers. But she shook 'em out, every damned one. She's raza, she's a person. And then, when you see how bright she is ... and lively, too. And let's not omit pretty, 'cause she is. And then when she carries all of that and turns out to be a nice kid, you can see, can't you? Can't you? I'm saying she stood on her two hind legs, straightened up her own panties, and told that Ira Escobar where to go. That's the door, cabrón. Your nose is in place, isn't it? Well, follow it out that door.

It'd be a comfort for me to see how that cabrón reacted when she blew up that perfect little world of his. And don't go thinking he didn't like to have Becky as a slave. Ha! The Leguizamóns are a right bunch of bastards—men and women. And then, when you add some Leyva blood to theirs? It gets worse. And worse because they turn into despots. Others come out crazier than crazy. There's Lourdes, for one, and no need to go on from there. As for those who don't come out babbling away, those turn out the worst: bullies, advantage-seekers, back stabbers ... and see these eyes here? Yeah, these I'm pointing to, you can use 'em as witnesses.

And good for Becky, say I. Two months, as I told you. Two whole

months of vacation is what I took. Two months away from this country
which is out of control, like a colt that's spat out its hackamore: no way
to guide it.

Two months in Bavaria, in Ulm—my Karl-Heinz's home. No, I'm
not a kid anymore, I said goodbye to menopause some years back, too,
but I do miss my red-headed German man. And because of him, and
because of his generosity, and the kind ways of his parents—I lived with
'em, you know, my in-laws, and I did so till they died. And for all of
that, I had, needed, wanted to go back.

It was for old times' sakes, sure. A sentimental journey. Me. But
Ulm had changed. Noisier. And the river that goes by it was filthy, sick,
oily with waste and garbage ... But it had been home for me.

Earlier, the year I buried Günther, my father-in-law, Manfred Rommel, was the mayor in Stuttgart, and he came to the funeral. He shook
my hand, stood by me. He was the son of General Rommel. But what
did I know about Rommel? Nothing, nothing then, and nothing now,
either .... The one Rommel I did know was that kid, the grandson of
Epigmenio Salazar, you remember Epigmenio? Didn't work a single
solitary day in his life; left all of that to his wife .... But this Rommel,
well, he must be in his forties by now.

Yes, back to Ulm. The house I lived in, the one I sold, is now an
apartment house. But the neighborhood? No change to speak of: you
can eat all three meals off the streets, it's that clean. But not as quiet
anymore, too many cars, motorcycles ... But the trip did me good.
I even got to see people who remembered me. Me! Die Mexicane.
'Cause that's what they called me.

But to tell the truth again, I never did take a liking to the language,
to the way it sounded. It was probably me, in the end. Couldn't make
heads or tails out of it. Oh, I could say this and that and my in-laws
understood me well enough. We'd laugh, all three of us, because I'd
call the things in the kitchen whatever I wanted to. At times, I'd just
point, and we'd laugh again.

I swear that the man who invented that language had nothing better
to do and so they drowned him in a beer vat. I could say guten morgen
all right, but with kissing the old folks, sharing our coffee and tea and
milk, and the quietness of it all, and love, above everything else, that,
love, I lived well and happy, too.

Then, when my mother-in-law, Helga, when she and I buried
Günther, we'd go to the park and take long walks. Then, on a Wednesday, every Wednesday, all of Ulm went to the cemeteries. Can you believe it? Like a day off. It was beautiful. All the cemeteries in the city,
full of flowers.

And so we'd walk and sit, enjoy each other's company. Oh, and

German television ... the absolute worst. Worse than ours. I swear it is. Helga would almost die laughing at me; no, there's no future for German television. But speaking of all those good people, my Karl-Heinz died in Pretoria, of a heart attack. And to think we had been there, in that concentration camp during the War, as a German, of all things! It's like a very strange dream, all of it.

I can almost laugh about it now, but not then. And then, after the war, when the Volkswagen Werke began to open up car agencies there, in South Africa, Karl-Heinz and I went back there.

And I'll tell you this: in the four-five years we lived there, in Pretoria, we kept a sharp lookout for a familiar face, a guard, a cook, something. Never did see one. Nothing.

But I don't, I don't dwell on it. And the life was harsh, cruel even ... but we survived to return to Germany at a time when there was no food in the cities. Those were dangerous times. And there was hunger, too. And five, six-year-old kids loaded up with firewood like little donkeys ...

Not now, of course. Now they're fat and rich, but back then, in '45, '46, '47 ... people would kill for a pound of potatoes .... Dangerous.

Karl-Heinz went right back to the diplomatic corps, but he couldn't take it; new people, he said, but no different from the Nazis. Just like them, he said, and that's what made it worse .... But he had connections still, and by '50, '51, Volks was off and running, and my Karl-Heinz taught me the business.

He'd say, "Viola, business is business—Geschafte ist Geschafte, algo así. Business is business, cars, machines, etcetera ... All the same. Don't drive the workers away, give the best service and even if you don't make as much, insist on the best service. The money'll come in soon enough."

Oh, he'd say other things, too, but it was the part about service, the attention to detail, that's what stuck to me.

And Becky knows. Saw it right off, she did. And she'd be in the money by now if she hadn't been such a little coward years ago and cut away from Ira. But those days are gone, and there she is: just as pretty, capable, talented, and no nonsense about her either. Able to go straight to the nub. Clear headed, cuts through the details, too. What can I say?

It's been a long day: a walk around the Barragán office building, a longish ride in Viola's car (driving at a steady clip and she waves here

and there to passersby), back to the office for work and a light me-
rienda of coffee and pan de dulce, and now it's time for a frosted glass
of limeade.

The listener senses—the listener feels this—that Viola is to finish up
a part of Becky's life—most likely another personal side to it—and then
send the listener on to other things.

And on that same note, what can I tell you about Becky and Jehu?
And where to start, too? Maybe it doesn't matter where I start .... Yes,
that's it. Maybe it doesn't matter at all, I mean about them, Becky and
Jehu ....

But there's always a but, and there is one thing that matters: to me,
that's of real concern, and here it is. Jehu is not a grueling bore, and
he is not bored either, and that's part of his secret life. His character,
personality.

And Ira? That poor devil: as bored as two pansy boys in a room
full of women or real men. Worse: Ira is not only a bore, he is boring.
And for me, to know this, you see, I've yet to say a word to that boy
since he's lived here in Klail. So, for me to know of that dull side of his
means he's got some fame going. And worse still again, and it doesn't
get any better, he's heavy handed with people. Lacks the touch, and he
doesn't know it. And yet, people will say, he can't be that way; why, the
man's a politician.

Tell you what: county commissioner is as high as he'll get. And then,
he'd not gotten that high if Noddy Perkins hadn't helped, and down he'll
come if Noddy ever gets his hemorrhoids in an uproar ....

After Becky's decision, I've no idea how it went for Ira at the Bank. I
mean, Jehu was there, and he's a great part of the Bank. It's just a good
thing, though, that Ira was transferred over to the Savings and Loan.

It couldn't have been easy on Jehu either; he gets no pleasure, none
at all, out of hurting people. An uncommon banker, that boy.

Of course, Noddy's no fool. That red-boned, freckle-faced son-of-
a-fruit-tramp wasn't born just the other day, you know. Too, keeping
Jehu at the Bank was plain good business: Jehu runs a good shop there.

That Jehu, ah, when was it? Five? Six, eight years ago, was it? When
he went after Becky? That's understandable. To be expected almost. At
first it was Plain Jane Sex, but as it is in everything else, he must've seen
what was there, in Becky.

I don't know this. I don't discuss sex with Jehu. I don't discuss his private life with him. We're friends, that boy and I, and I've got a weakness for smart people. I just figure he saw Becky, knew, intuited maybe, guessed right, something, that Becky had *médula*, as we say. Character. Substance. She was a person, and could be her own person, someday. See? Man was right.

About that time, Jehu was out like a cowboy, cutting and culling from the herd. But he fell off that quarterhorse of his. Livita. Livita San Esteban did it. And Jehu got serious. But we know what happened to Olivia, third-year in med school, some goddam drunk kills her ....

On the other side of the world, Becky sends Ira on his way, and with Jehu—a widowed-groom, really—I, yeah, me, and I admit it, too, I sort of got them, him and Becky, I sort of got them together.

I know it sounds like some play or opera the way I'm going on about it here, but it happened. Ira's line was cut off from the dock, and Becky kissed off that Music Club goodbye, too. Goodbye to all that. And goodbye to something else, too: all manner of strings.

Although Elvira Navarrete and I are friends, old friends, and we've weathered storms and hurricanes here in the Valley ... and I'll tell you that when Becky weaned herself off her mamma's breast, she did it consciously. That was some decision, that was.

And it was, and let me tell you why: it takes a lot of damn nerve, fiber, spine, good, old-fashioned Mexican Valley guts not to knuckle to—get this—to what people will say. I'm an expert on "what people will say," that qué dirá la gente claptrap. You're talking to one of the world's biggest targets here; used to be I walked around with a target on my back. Here, hit this; yeah.

Of course, people who knew nothing, had no blood interest in any of Becky's doings, had one thing: malice and an opinion, or a set of them. Sure, and if you have the time, they'd say, I'll give it to you, here and now. It was something to do, something to get them through another hot summer. Entertainment, even.

It was the same when I married Harmon Gillette, years ago. Oh, sure. And really, who could've given a damn about that? And still, they talked. It wasn't their business, but as in business and politics, many talkers, few doers. One does deserve to go to heaven for all the chances one takes on earth, and for putting up with the Ira Escobars of the world.

Example: If I know of someone who's destined for heaven it's Blanca Rivera, the Presbyterian, Pioquinto's widow. Pioquinto and I had our motel workouts up and down the Valley. When he died, Blanca had a few pennies saved, not many. Their home? Modest but paid for. Bills? Few, nothing serious. Kids? Zero. So? Well, a year or so later, I took her on as cashier at my first Shopping Bags store. Here, in Klail.

When the business increased, I opened up another one, and Blanca handled that one, too. And now we're up to seventeen stores across Belken County, run by Blanca Rivera, widow of Reyes, and that's how she still signs for everything, bookkeeper, manager; she orders, everything, eh?

Just like Becky. I started her on the Busy Bee Burgers and from there to the three movie drive-ins, which I've just converted into flea markets. Becky it was who said to close the drive-ins. Shut 'em up, she said. Profits in the Flea Markets, she says. We can rent out three hundred stalls there, sell the speakers for scrap ... Well, turned out we got four hundred stalls, but the decision was a right one.

And I know what you're thinking about Blanca. Did she know about Pioquinto and me. She did 'cause I told her a year after he died at the Holiday Inn we'd been at.

Blanca said then she maybe suspected something was up, but that she didn't know what it was exactly.

Now? Now she even laughs and does so because she figured out why Pioquinto went on the hunt. She kept him on short rations, and Pioquinto—forty plus years—wanted a hump at least once a day. His death over to the Holiday Inn was really something to laugh about ...

Oh, I know that sounds cold, but mark this down: Blanca needed help, money to live on, and I took her on. I'm not talking about a guilty conscience here. Two people out of four billion doing what Pioquinto and I did? That's a sin? Making each other happy?

Sha! Blanca needed help, and guess what? Pioquinto must've taught her bookkeeping, accounting, even. I think numbers are a God-given talent, something Pro-vi-den-tial, as she says in that Presby way of hers. That Blanca ...

∴ Viola hired Becky + is supporting of her

And that is Viola Barragán, one of Becky's friends. A glance at the listener's wristwatch shows it's 8:15 p.m. September, and the sun is still up there and beating down at 95 degrees Fahrenheit in the Rio Grande Valley, Belken County, Texas.

The listener dreams of a cold shower and enters the house without bothering to turn on the lights; they'd only add to the heat. There's some TV blather about a possible veering of the hurricane out in the Gulf; it just may hit the Valley. Possible and may. Words.

Tomorrow? A conversation with Isidro Peralta.

Isidro Peralta

It's Isidro Peralta's turn at bat. The survivor of identical twins; an electrician by trade; their father, also an electrician, lives in one of the only three houses on that triple lot. The other houses belong to Eugenio Peralta's widow and to the informant. The families share one common mail box, and this calls for an explanation:

Eugenio, dead these four years now, left two surviving sons: Eugenio Jr., 20, and Isidro II, 18. For his part, Isidro also has two sons: Isidro Jr., 20, and Eugenio, 18.

The Star Route drivers who deliver the mail threw their hands in the air years ago, and hence the common rural mail box.

The listener called ahead and after the usual mix-up of names of sons and cousins, the listener made an appointment with the surviving twin.

Yep, if my brother Eugenio were alive today, he'd be forty-years-old, same age as me; we was twins. Got killed by a brick thrown by God Himself, yessir. That brick fell from heaven itself, wasn't a man-thrown brick at all.

He and I was working on an electrical job for Viola Barragán in that office building of hers. Started off with two and then she went on and added two more floors to make it four.

Well, it was right there where the Silva brothers, and Chago Leal, and the two of us won the first big contract to wire up the rest of that office building, and we all made a profit, you bet.

Doña Viola doesn't want shit—that's cheap wire and cheaper labor —on her property. What I'm saying is she wanted copper, not aluminum wiring. Aluminum is good and cheap but treacherous. Won't last. Copper will, though. Copper'll go through Hell itself. You can't beat copper.

The Doña is exigente. Always the best 'cause it's also the cheapest, as she sees it. And that damned brick was the best, too. That's Double-duty Fire-Up—you with me? First quality goods and made here, on this side of the Rio Grande.

Now, you're going to find a lot of Texas Anglos in the construction trades who use Mexican brick—and it's good, too —but here in Belken County, all over the Valley, there are Texas mexicanos who know how to make brick; best there is. The Munguilla brothers for starters. Or the Morales family—the ones with the funeral house and the kilns—what do you say to that?

And I do miss my bro. But he always had bad luck, you know. Born but with one testicle, just like me, a ciclán, as we say. Oh, well ....

As for Jehu, we've known him ... well, it's only me now, but I've known him since school. He was raised, protected by the Buenrostro family. They're kin, and he and Rafe Buenrostro are close, tight, always have been. You fought one, you had to fight the other, been that way since school.

Rafe's father was don Jesús Buenrostro, El Quieto. I didn't know the man, he was a grown-up, see? But he took in Jehu Malacara. What I'm telling you is what I got from my father. Yeah ... knew don Quieto, I mean, don Jesús. And my dad, he knew the brother, too, don Julián, the father of Melchor who God keeps etcetera ...

About Jehu—God's truth—he's always treated me fairly and more than fair sometimes. I've never been in the position of doing him a favor, but I'm ready whenever and whatever.

Sometime back, once, can't remember where or when, but once, someone told me that Jehu had bedded down Rebecca Escobar. What I'm saying here is rumor, okay? You asked and all I'm only saying is what I know or heard ....

Anyway. That he grabbed her by the ears and let's head for the open Gulf, the breeze is up and all that. But do I know this for a fact? For a fact? No.

But if the subject was Sammie Jo Perkins, that's a different matter. And I wasn't the only one who knew? Get me?

As for Olivia San Esteban, that was a sad piece of business. Serious, too. Here, in this case, Jehu went about it serious, formal. As my dad says: he settled down, he grew up, asentó cabeza, you know? Now, Jehu didn't quit going to the Blue Bar or over to Dirty Barrón's Aquí Me Quedo Bar, but he cut the rest of the stuff, the running around. Like a bullfighter, he cut off his pony tail, or like a boxer who hangs 'em up.

Got serious for once and then for what? So that some dumb pinche drunken bolillo come and broadside her? So he can kill her in a second, just about? Son-of-a-bitch run a red light out at the Military turn off, and him on one of those goddam outsized pickups. Shit.

Olivia San Esteban didn't live those ten days in the hospital; she was in a coma. And Jehu? From his house to work and then to the hospital. Yessir. He was serious. When Olivia died and was buried, Jehu had to go on living; no choice. But he had his health. And he'd changed, no doubt about that.

Oh, he dated La Chacha—Irene Paredes—the one that does things with science; something. Well, she works there at the Court House, where Rafe works, you know: Jehu's cousin.

But as for Irene, Jehu didn't go out much or long either. A year? And then, de repente, just like that, he marries Rebecca Escobar, living together, making or keeping a family. Why, that was like heat thunder to me, flat out of the blue and bam!

It was too fast for me to follow, I'll tell you that. La Escobar set Mr. Commissioner adrift like a shrimp trawler with no nets to drag .... I hear she chucked him out of the house. That's tough, right? That's what people say.

I don't know those people, the Escobars. They belong to another class of people, I'd say. But if you're talking social classes, that cuts little to no ice with Jehu. For him, one standard, everyone's the same, in or out of the Bank; he's a fair one that Jehu, you got to say that for him.

Now, it can't be more than two years ago, I don't think—talking about the San Esteban girl's death. La Escobar boots her husband right in the ass, and begins her life with the kids in that house of theirs. I think Chago Leal, maybe Arnold Tucker, got the wiring contract for that one.

One thing for sure: Rebecca Escobar isn't going to starve to death, and then, all of a sudden, you just didn't see her pictures in the Enterprise-News. Yeah. And she used to be in it, a lot, with the Women's this and the Women's that, you know.

Well, on a Palm Sunday morning I think it was, there's this car parked in front of her house. And that's a No Parking zone, too. To back up just a bit, she'd got me to install two air-conditioning units, one for the kitchen and one for the glassed-in porch. I drove up that Sunday morning after Mass, and there was the car. Up front. You know what I'm saying here?

Well, it was Jehu's car. A Bank car, yeah. Can you beat that? Well, here I was, rewiring the two rooms, replacing hot plugs with a ground on 'em, one-day job. Top.

And Jehu? In shirt sleeves. Happy as a cat in a barn full of mice.

That cabrón ... No! That's just an expression; Jehu is not a cabrón. Oh no, he's far from being an asshole. No, no. That would be the last word for Jehu Malacara.

But there he was: at home. He spotted me working in the kitchen, nodded and that was it. No malice in that nod, no winking of the eye either. It was a greeting. Well, that wasn't none of my business. I mean, what did I have to do with any of that? My old man did not set out to raise idiots. Jehu was there and Jehu was there, and he sure didn't ask permission from Isidro Peralta, master electrician.

'Cause that's what I am, a master electrician, and I was hired for that, and I did the work on time. A clean house, the kids happy and laughing with their Mom, all the time I was there, and if Rebecca wasn't bothered by my comings and goings, well, I ask you: Why should I be bothered, or care?

So it's got to be two years 'cause that's when Ira was made secretary, manager, something like that, over to Klail Savings. And then, some six months after that, the same job over to Jonesville—the Escobars are originally from Jonesville. They're not from Klail. Rebecca is a Cogwell, something like that. Her father was a soldier; Anglo, and married to a monied woman, one with property. She was a Narváez or a Navarro. No, no, no, no not either one at all. She's a Navarrete; yeah. Old don Julio's daughter, 'cause there was money there ...

Later, Chago Leal told me this was so. Years and years ago, Chago was an apprentice for an old alky named Willis here in Klail who owned another shop in Jonesville. Well, according to Chago, the Navarrete's decided to re-wire the entire house, top to bottom, north to south, okay? Takes money for that. Old Parr Willis got the contract, and that's how Chago Leal got inside that house. A house-and-a-half is what Chago used to say.

So, this Rebecca is part of that family. And, between you and me, I didn't know a pharmacist could make that kind of money .... Maybe they do, but old don Celso Villalón used to say that anything is possible, and that contraband is easier than working for a living.

That aside, that house was a well-made house. Solid. And that's why the wiring took time. No sheet rock there, no sir. Chago Leal says that after that job, that big a contract, he wasn't scared of any job, anywhere.

He earned his journeyman badge right there.

It should be pointed out that Isidro Peralta received three phone calls, gave out two estimates, and wrote a message on a pink pad. Later, one of his sons brought the mail, already sorted, no doubt.

At that time, Rebecca must've been in college, the university. Here in the state, yeah, but Up North somewhere. Near Dallas.

As for Klail City, she and Ira Escobar landed here some nine-ten years ago. Oh! About the time he became a politician real sudden like ... well, it was about that time that Jehu was a good friend to Noddy Perkins's daughter ... and she married for a second time, too.

I'm telling you, that Jehu was a piece of work. But there he is, married to Rebecca by a judge, so what do I know? One thing's sure, they sure as hell don't have to give me an accounting for their life together. Everyone has their one life to lead, right?

But this I got to say: there, where you see Jehu, and he's a good person, too, well anyway, like that, quiet, peaceful like, just like his cousin, Rafe. I wouldn't want to tangle with either one. Not bigmouths, either one. Goodness, when do they ever act tough? But I'd pass on some advice to anyone who doesn't know Jehu, that it's best not to crowd him.

Easy going, playful, name it, but it's like the Anglos say, "He's always holding back. Something in reserve."

And then, he doesn't hold grudges either. No grudges to hold when you don't take shit from anyone. And like I said, one standard, in or out of the Bank, and everyone's equal.

Weeeeelll, living with or married, don't matter to me which, Rebecca Escobar—or Malacara maybe—she's a person, and good at business. She runs some of Viola Barragán's Business, and I'm a witness. And Viola won't cheat you either and Rebecca's the same. Yessir.

Piece work, a big job, big contractor, little contractor—everyone gets respect. Viola's not like some—like a lot, and raza, too—that only gives the big jobs to the Anglos— Klail Electric, Belken & Co—and the little jobs to us, as if we didn't know as much as anyone. Bunch-a raza shits.

Tell you what I also like about doña Viola Barragán. She works with attorneys—contracts, deadlines, bonuses, everything. Take me, I can buy on credit or she'll give it to me: whatever I need and it's "Call me if you need anything." You listening?

I didn't mean to veer off here, but it also has to do with Jehu: If you go to the Bank on business, it doesn't matter how you're dressed. That's right. You go in there, sit in his office, explain to him what you'd like to do, and he listens. He knows how to ask questions, hard questions. Then he starts with the figures. He advises you. Yeah. That cabrón, he ... I mean, he knows his business.

And he doesn't give a good goddammit if your name's Juan Lanas, Pepe Cabras, or Bruno Shafter of Belken & Co. or even Junior McQueen from Klail Electric. All treated the same: courtesy, seriousness, and if you know what you're talking about, the loan is as good as yours. Right there, dammit. Right then. The man has confidence in you, yeah. And he handles big deals, yessir.

Let me tell you this. Chago Leal and I went into a temporary partnership, limited, eh? We partnered on an estimate for a job with doña Viola. Rebecca Escobar was there too.

I'm going to stop here to tell you that La Escobar is a very beautiful woman. Not bonita, pretty, but linda. Bella, even. Beautiful. And, to work with doña Viola, she's got to be sharp as good vinegar. But she better be intelligent, too, since doña Viola isn't selling newspapers on some street corner; there's money in that company. Rebecca Escobar's got to be a good one.

And you can't take her looks away, she's got 'em. You know what else? Olivia San Esteban was a beauty. And yet, they didn't look alike, did they? I mean, Rebecca Escobar's eyes are brown[1], biggish somewhat, and round. The nose is a bit small for me, and kind-a pale, too, but that coal-tar hair helps. Her ... her figure, ah, nice, real nice.

The San Esteban girl? Different. Pretty and a lot. But like the old days somehow. You know what I mean? I remember her eyes, sort of washed out: gray? The mouth a bit wide, but a great smile. I fell for her at Klail High, but she never knew ... No one knew, not even my brother, I want you to know. My twin! I never told him, he never knew.

Olivia's hair was as black as Rebecca's, but longer, shiny, and then that face. That skin, like a smooth, skinned almond. Yeah. That Ollie San Esteban was special. A little on the thin side for me, but not bony, no. There's a better word for it, but what do I know?

Well, the thing was our contract—Chago Leal's and mine with doña Viola—brought us to Rebecca Escobar. She already knew who I was and said hi and shook my hand and all. Like I said, she's got to be a sharp one to work for someone like doña Viola. Well, right away she told us to leave the pick ups where they were, and she got us in her car.

And how long was the job going to take, she asked. The hot plugs this and the tubing that, the lighting and the wattage, what carpenter would we recommend; just like the owner of any other shop or store.

---

[1]Note: Becky Malacara's husband, the banker Jehu, corraborates the color of his wife's eyes. This may not be important, but The Listener, in going over P. Galindo's papers, read where P. Galindo says they are green.

She carried the two little green books, just like ours: how much, where, and there she'd go with that hand calculator just like Chago and me. Business, yessir.

A rosebud is what she is. And we're talking a big job here when she said right out, "Well, what do you figure you need to start? How much money are we talking about?"

Yeah. A line of credit.

Well, first off, she was going to open a special account for us at the Bank. We could draw from it, just sign for the materials. A big, fat contract all drawn up. And all the time, cool, nice, and then guess what? I realized I had my mouth hanging open ...

And here I always thought she was a pushover you know. I mean, I'd had a few dealings with Ira Escobar at the Bank. He was like a flat tire, no air to him.

I don't know what happens north of the Valley, like up in Austin or China and Europe, but when it comes to my craft, I can tell you chapter and verse about what I do. Ira? I never got the impression he was all there. Kind of goofy. Silly. A waste of time to talk to that guy, because I'd wind up talking to Noddy or Jehu, one. First with Noddy and then with Jehu or straight to Jehu.

Man, if I ran my shop like that, I'd've closed up by now or worse than that, my dad would've taken a stick to me, make that a BIG stick, for being so dumb.

And the guy's a county commissioner? That guy? Man, if they're all like that up at the Court House, they better change the wiring, quick.

But back to Rebecca. She wasn't out to make a big deal out of this. If there was something she didn't know, she'd pop a question. Say she'd see something different from the way we'd see it, she's say something. But not like she was trying to show you up, not like some others.

It was negocio, man. Business.

And the way she trusted you, too, and her own ways of doing, saying things ... I think that's why she and Jehu get along so well. Got to be.

But as I've been saying all along, I don't swim in those waters, at all. Now I'll see Jehu at the Blue Bar, like I said, 'cause he is the way he is, a natural. He doesn't claim to know everything, and you'll see him sitting and talking and listening to the old men, los viejitos. Men like Chago Leal's dad, or Garrido, or Dirty Barron himself, and old Echevarría when he used to hold court there. And sometimes he drops in with Rafe, hellos all around, one or the other will stand a round, but that's plain old friendship. We're not talking of acting like a big shot or buying rounds like politicians.

At other times, you won't see him there for weeks at a time. But he shows up, sticks around.

So he and Rebecca they both got their jobs ... Like that one we did for doña Viola, where we came out just fine: we finished that office building, the city inspector passed on it, and then the county guy, Solís, I think his name is, he signed away on it too. It was a good job, and we guaranteed it, every time. Well, when we worked on one of the old stores and on one of the new ones, which we finished ten days ahead of schedule, and both inspectors gave their okays again, doña Viola drove up to my shop, parked her car and in she comes, handing me a five-hundred dollar check! Had one for Chago, too. So how do you think we felt? Right! And know what we did then? Passed some of the bonus money to the two apprentices. Made me feel pretty good too.

It was good business, I know that, and Rebecca Escobar—and I guess I better start calling her Rebecca Malacara, right? Anyway, she was there with doña Viola a little while later and shook our hands. Business.

Sure, good business.

Andrés Malacara

Andrés Malacara, in his maturity. A man in his high eighties now and sitting under a chinaberry tree on a straight back chair. A terry cloth towel across his lap, a cover against the sun when he walks around and also used for shooing off blue-bottle flies. He's putting the finishing touches on some pink grapefruit wine, and he watches it drip into an aluminum vat as the listener comes up.

Been expecting you. Dirty Barron said you'd be dropping by ... Well, let's get to it.

You and I both know that a lot of Valley people share blood kinships. Not many idiots around, though, and that's 'cause we don't mix except every three generations or so. Been going on since 1749, and here I am, eighty-two, and I heard that from my maternal grandfather, Juan Nepomuceno Vilches.

First cousins don't marry, and like I said, it's too close to the blood. Now, that some come out slow-like or dull as cast iron, it's because their folks was dumb to begin with. But idiocy, no, not from crossing the bloods.

I will say, though, that crossing and top crossing of blood is good for the breed. Same thing happens out in the pastures where I was born, the Toluca Ranch.

I'm eighty-two, on the nose; the twenty-third of March, Santo Toribio's day, and today, April fourth, Day of Santo Isidoro, marks an even dozen, twelve years to the day, when we buried Esteban Echevarría. If he were here, alive, today, that'd be the man who could tell you everything. Todo. From A to Z. Yes.

I don't have the gift, and I sure don't know as much as he did, but I've got more than three-quarters of a century on me, so I must know something about the old families, las viejas familias.

When you called, you mentioned the Barragán family, but that's not an old family. Telésforo Barragán and his wife landed here around 1920 or so. An old family is a different matter.

I'll give you an example. The Leguizamón bunch got here after the end of the Civil War. They got to the border, to the southern bank of the Rio Grande, about 1857, maybe '58. But they didn't come over during the Civil War, no sir. They were across, making money: cotton, smuggling firearms, war stuff, food, you name it.

Those families are old, but they're not what we call old families or what old Echevarría called familias viejas. Now, the Cano family and the Guzmáns, and the Rincón, the Buenrostro and Malacara families, and the Vilches, the Tueros. Them. Those are the old families. Yours, see? Me, I'm a Tuero on my maternal grandmother's side, doña Esther Tuero.

The Navarrete family, to give you another instance, dropped here when this part of the world became the Republic of Texas; 1840, '42, I'd say. My grandmother Esther was becoming a señorita around that time—she was 15 or so—and she first met them then.

And Esteban Echevarría used to tell me ... oh, Esteban's father, don Hilarión, he was a little old red-faced man about the size of a shoe tack. Had all his hair, too, and white as burro milk ... Anyway, Esteban used to tell me that the first skirmishes, the feud, between the first Buenrostros and the Leguizamóns came about on account of the Leguizamóns allying themselves with the Anglos crowding in here way back then. The Leguizamóns also sided with the army, yeah, the old Confederates. And with some raza, too, up the River ... Laredo, those parts ...

The governor of Texas had enough on his plate around that time and the Valley and its people suffered on account of that. He couldn't tend to us ... Ha!

Listen, the Sedition of 1915 was a result of all that way back then. To begin with, the Rangers had lorded it over us since my century, the one I was born in, the nineteenth. Yes. They took heavy advantage after 1915 as well, and they'd go around scaring people using, boots, pistols, and shotguns, in the elections in the 1920s and the '30s, too. Shoot, in certain parts of the Valley, up to the '50s. Yeah. Can you picture that? Yesterday, you might say.

No, the seditious ones of '15 rose up and rebelled because la raza was up there with the Rangers and with their goddam guns and shootings.

But there were raza turncoats, too. Traitors. Oh, yes. And the Anglos later betrayed them. Ha, that'll teach you to leave the nest, cabrones.

So it was around there that the Buenrostro-Leguizamón bad blood first showed and flowed. Later, when don Jesús Buenrostro, El Quieto, was murdered, two Leguizamóns were taken care of, dealt with. The two Mexican nationals who murdered El Quieto, well, they were also dispatched around the same time.

Javier Leguizamón always claimed that he had nothing to do with any of that. It got to be embarrassing after a while, all that denying. He said it once and he repeated it a thousand times. Embarrassing. Got to the point where he believed it. That's really something, isn't it?

Ha! He and Angelita didn't have any kids, like me and my wife and maybe for the same reason, too. We both married good women, but we ran around a lot ... For my part, I know I strewed four out of marriage, three boys and a girl. And I saw to them, yes I did, and all four chose my name later on. All legal.

My wife ... I buried her over there, see that cemetery yonder, by the flume? That's our cemetery. A lot of Cano folk there, Guzmáns, too, and Malacaras, of course. Esteban Echevarría was supposed to have been buried there, but the Buenrostros said Echevarría'd be buried with them, at the Carmen Ranch.

That was young Buenrostro's doing, Rafe, and of the three Buenrostro men, Rafe took after his dad a bit more than the other two, Aaron and Mailo. We're talking of three full men here, and Rafe, the middle son, he's something else ...

As for the Leguizamóns, what can I tell you? Back in the 1920s, like I said, the '30s, too, before some American company came and ate up every creamery and dairy farm hereabouts, they'd already had their dealings with the Leguizamón family.

And when I had to deal with the Americans, I dealt in spot cash. No checks, no thank you, sir. A bank had skinned my friends and had skinned me too like an eggshell, back in '31 and from then on I said, "No checks." It was either cash or I'd dump the milk in the garbage pails, since that's what the banks had turned my accounts to, garbage.

To this day and until tomorrow, if I die then, I'll go to my grave with one belief: those damn bankers told their friends what it was that was going to happen. Hell, yes. And us? You know what we got? We got a big fat nothing with zeroes on it. Hmph.

So as I said, they had to pay me in cash and, since there were no other mouths to feed at home except my wife Aurelia's and mine, I was all right. All smiles and cash, yessir.

Javier Leguizamón is, was, a great uncle to Ira Escobar, the county commissioner. Don't know the boy, but he can't possibly amount to much; he's got some Leyva blood on his mother's side, and that's no help.

Protected by Javier? Absolutely. Spoiled, too, I'd say. And he's a banker, I hear. As I said, I've never met him. Oh, I've seen him here and there at some farm or ranch barbecue ... 'cause I don't go to no town barbecues. Klail or Flora, one. Won't go near any town. I'm a river man, a dairy man, and this is where you're going to find me dead tomorrow, next week, whenever.

No, I don't go into town. At all. I was well-served when I owned them two gaming houses in Klail. But when I left them, thirty years ago and more I came here, to these forty acres, and that's all anyone would want.

If I want to know what's going on, all I got to do is ask. But that's about it, 'cause if you want to find me, I'll be down by the River, fishing. So who wants to live in town, I ask you?

There's too many diseases in town. The water? On iron or plastic pipes, and then they run it through again, they reuse it. Not for me. Give me rainwater from the Gulf, the Rio Grande, and the lakes out here. And I boil it, too, and then I add half a spoonful of salt for every ten gallons, helps the digestion.

And what does one get out of living in town, anyway? Diseases! In thirty years now, this country of theirs has been in half-a-dozen wars, hasn't it? And what for? The Germans? Friends again. The Japanese? Same damn thing. And the dead? Dead.

Look, the world is no different from Belken County politics. You scratch mine, I'll scratch yours, and amen.

And there can't be anything filthier than a town, and I'm just sorry I didn't know any better when I first married. That's right. These last thirty-years have been the healthiest, sanest years of my life. Absolutely.

The listener was prepared for the above. It's one of Andrés Malacara's set pieces, but he means every word of it.

He's also an expert whittler and prefers the retama tree, but the mesquite will do, he says.

Time for a walk, and Andrés Malacara, with the listener in tow, walks toward the River. The farm lies two miles from the pumping station that draws its water from the Rio Grande. Half of the land has been saved for feed grass for his jerseys and black-and-whites.

Since you're here, I'll tell you that my nephew, Manuel Avila, was here day before yesterday. You know him? He's sandy-haired. Green-eyed. Much, much older'n you; he's close to fifty, I'd say. And talking about the divorce as you were, he was the one who brought the news here two, three years ago ...

That the Leguizamón-Leyva and the Navarrete families were all a-bother. That this was going on, that that was going on. A lot of noise, but for nothing from what I could see. And Manuel crying real tears 'cause he was laughing so hard.

Those families carried on he said. Aired a lot of clothing in public ... Whatever happened to shame in the Valley? Manuel just laughed away and kept saying, "So what?" And he'd laugh and say, "Well? Was the Queen of Prussia pregnant? Did she give birth? Who the hell cares?"

Manuel'd say, "Nothing to it, Uncle, just one more divorce," but there they were, acting as if we'd dropped another atomic bomb some-where." And Manuel was right. It was nothing. Ira Escobar's wife left him, pure and simple, that's all.

I can talk about that girl 'cause I know her and I know all her kind. To start off, her maternal grandfather, Julio Navarrete, was a gambler, and he also had shady businesses here and there. Half-hidden, you might say. He was also anybody's errand boy at the start of this century and later on he became a pharmacist. But I ask you, what did that piece of half-digested shit know about filling out a prescription?

First he opened up a drug store out to Flora—no, I'm wrong there. First Bascom, then Flora. Right. But a pharmacist ... shoot, not even the Anglos had licenses back then, not in the Valley they didn't. And then again, maybe that was it. Julio Navarrete probably said to himself, "Here's where I get mine." Yeah, that was probably it.

But when he first came to the Valley, starving, he was a gambler. Now, the first gaming house I opened up was near Relámpago, and that was in 1897, and I was nineteen-years-old then. How do you like that?

That's right, I had my own gambling place, and I got the money from a loan made me by my uncle Daniel Estudillo.

So Julio Navarrete came here as a gambler, and he was good, the sum-bitch. From gambler to part time whore-master: he ran some women here and there. After that, came the pharmacy, then the two dance hall-cantinas, and he kept them for forty years, and that's the truth.

He opened a whorehouse in Flora, and that was a big place, people said.

But all undercover, except the drug store. He was a family man, decent. Ha! He was nothing of the kind; he was a hypocrite. That was dirty money, and for some sixty years or so, I think he also might've cheated when he gambled. I never caught him at it, but if I had, I'd-a broken both his hands and all his fingers and knuckles for him. He might have known what I was capable of, and maybe that's why he didn't cheat at my place ... But who's to know, right?

Well, there it was, dirty money, made in secret. Smuggling? Why not? Smuggling's not the most difficult business in the world, and not on this border of ours; no, not when you've got relatives on both sides of the River. Easiest thing going, and you don't need any talent for that.

When Julio Navarrete died—that was out to Jonesville—I learned of it from Manuel, my nephew. As for Esteban Echevarría, all he said was, "Just one more down the chute, that's all."

Echevarría it was who told me of the dance-hall cantinas and the other stuff. Esteban knew a lot of secrets; took a lot of history with him when he died. Good person, Esteban.

Yeah ... these forty acres of mine are in Ira Escobar's precinct, you know. And it must be going on six years now, around election time it was, some flunky of his showed up here. That the county commissioner wanted to know if I needed anything, if I needed a favor done, he said. That if there was anything that he, the commissioner,could do for me.

Like what? I asked the flunky who showed up.

He answered in a flash: that the commissioner was ready and willing to pave the road leading to my gate from the highway, see? And beyond the gate, right up to my front door if I wanted it.

"Paved?" I asked him.

Yessir.

I told him no. I thanked him all right, but no thanks.

Told him I liked the smell of dirt when the rain wets it down, and I'd just as soon keep it that way.

Do you know that old boy wouldn't believe me? So I had to insist, convince him. What I didn't tell him was that I didn't want every S.O.B. dropping in whenever he felt like it. Those paved roads smell like cities to me, brings 'em in closer.

This way, when it rains, that black Valley mud'll keep an army away. So it was no, no thank you, no, Commissioner.

He was a young guy, the boy who came over, and all he did was scratch his head. In amazement, I'd say. Probably was the first damn time someone didn't want, didn't need something, from the commissioner.

That you come here, to talk, is one thing. You're family, that's enough for me ...

But that's about the closest I've come to dealing with that family.

My nephew Manuel Avila tells me that Jehu's back at the Bank after some sort of absence. You know, Esteban Echevarría sure was right about Jehu ... liked him, liked what he saw in him. Jehu is one of our Malacaras, but he's also a Vilches and a Tapia to boot. Those are good people, they're from El Ranchito, just east of Relámpago, past Los Indios.

I knew Jehu's parents, both of them. Died young, both of them. She went first. Her name was Tere, and once, when there wasn't one single penny in that house, she went to town, to Klail, to work as a maid. A domestic. Those were hard times. She didn't last long though. Couldn't stand to live in a town, and she didn't like city ways either.

And Jehu? Turned out solid. His Buenrostro cousins had a hand in that. And I did too. When my wife and I still lived in Klail, I had Jehu working for me at one of my gambling places. That boy was She-Arp. Honest, too, just like all the Malacaras. Wouldn't touch a penny.

One of my sons—he first used the last name Loera from his mother—he used to say that Jehu was straighter than a cedar post. How do you like that? Oh, one can learn to be honest, but you got to have some good blood in you, for starters. Jehu was the only birth out of that Vilches-Malacara blood, but it was a good mix. Yessir.

But there's always bad luck somewhere. His novia, that girl he loved, got herself killed in a car wreck, according to Manuel. Like I been telling everybody left and right, cities are going to be the death of everyone. They're dangerous, I know what I'm talking about. You won't catch me there ...

The listener spent two days and nights at don Andrés Malacara's farm. The man was proven correct: eight hours of hard rain made it impossible for the listener to leave, or, as don Andrés saw it, the rain also kept the townies from coming in.

Emilio Tamez

Emilio Tamez, in the crucible. Works for the Klail-Blanchard-Cooke Ranch. Factotum says it all for this informant. Brother to the late Ernesto Tamez, killed in the bar called Aquí me Quedo, owned and operated for years by the listener's uncle, Lucas Barrón, el Chorreao. Tamez walks with a limp, the result of a childhood accident.

I can tell you all there is to know about divorces. I'll say I can. Been through one myself, with Esthercita Monroy.

Let me tell you this: you end up with a woman like Esthercita, you better give 'em a golden bridge to walk away from you, yessir. Pave the way for 'em, give 'em distance, and then get the hell away from them.

That's what I did, followed my own prescription, yessir. She got to acting like a Ranch foreman and I just brought me some new rope. Here! I said, run with it. There's the door to this house, take off.

Ira Escobar did the very rightest thing when he got shed of Becky. Now I'm not saying Esthercita and Becky belong to the same rank in society. Becky, she comes from folks who are comfortable, she's a woman of possibles, money, eh? That aside, Becky and Esther could be twins. They both think they're independent. ⸺

I've always thought it kind-a crazy for a woman to run a man. That's a sure way to end bad!

And just like I told you, Ira was righter than right; he knew where the door was and how to open the damn thing. Sí, señor. Sí. Sí. I'd see Becky out there at the Cooke Ranch, and she'd be all decked out, nice and all, with Ira's money of course, oh sure, tailor-mades, pleats here and there.

You'd-a thought she was a queen or something. Una reina. And when I say the money belonged to Ira, I'm on target, oh, yeah. Why, even the dumbest chickens, roosters, and pullets know the Navarretes are the meanest, stingiest people anyone ever came across. Made that way, you see. Why, every President Lincoln penny they ever got has turned green by now. Yeah, that's why they got all their money. But it ain't all that much either, don't you see? Oh, they may brag they got money, but where do they ever show it off? Nah. They wouldn't spend a penny until the whole family took a vote on it.

But Ira isn't like that at all. He's a faithful husband, an honest politician, and there's damn few a-them. He's a ... a ... a man of honor is what he is. Sobriety, seriousness, that's what you'll find in the Escobar family flag, yessiree. And related to the Leguizamóns and to the Leyvas, too. The Leyva blood also comes from his mother's side o-things. Ira got the best of everything in that bargain.

And he's got learning, too. He and I are about the same age, but he got to go to Texas A & M University, the military school which is bettern'n the other one. And, he also got to enroll at St. Mary's, which is in the city of San Antonio. Yes. Right. That ought to tell you something, says it all, doesn't it? Are there, can there be two better colleges or universities better than those two in the entire United States and Mexico? The answer to that is no, right?

Old Ira, man, he just tightened up his belt and told Becky, straight out, that she could damn well choose: you stay, and I'm still the boss, like always, and we'll have peace around here and outside too. Otherwise, it's a divorce. Just like that. Tough.

Well, she sure thought she could play around with Ira. Ho! Couldn't read him at all, a-tall. But that's her beeswax ...

And I did the very same thing with Esthercita Monroy. I was up to here, you understand? Whatever else you may think, or might've heard, the Monroys like to throw their weight around, and my brother-in-law, Raúl? ... he's at the very top o' the list.

Can you even imagine that? Ha! So what happens? First male child we had, we just had to call him Raúl, nothing else but. I ask you, just what the hell kind of a name is Raúl, anyway? It's nothing, it's ordinary, it's a name like a day of the week; anybody can be named Raúl, you know that? Sure.

I wanted the first boy to be named after me, Emilio. The first born, right? And then we could call him Junior. Oh, no. Raúl, that's what the Monroys wanted, and Esthercita led the parade on that one, sure she did.

And that's where it all started. She won that fight, and I gave in, and that's what one gets for being a nice person. Let that be a lesson to all

... and that's how one pays for one's errors. But that's water over the Falcon Dam, and the best thing you can do is to let it drift down and out to the Gulf, as the old folks say.

... But you see, that type of woman, and it is a type, they always run short on shame. They haven't got enough of it. Here's what I'm talking about: What did Becky Escobar turn around and do? Did she pack up and go to her folks' home in Jonesville? Did she go out there and start raising the kids? Hell, no.

I don't see how she did it, where it was she went to find all the damn nerve in the world, but she stayed in Ira's house. You ever seen nerve like that before? I bet you haven't, have you? I sure as all Hell haven't, not if I lived for a hundred years in every county in the state of Texas.

And Ira? All class that boy. The house? It's yours, he says. Keep it, keep it and raise the kids in the best there is. That's what's called a sense of honor, of doing what is right! And that's having the balls to do it. Ah, sorry. Takes guts.

To take care a-the house like God orders, yeah, and then? When bad luck follows bad, you got a heap of very big trouble there. Becky and her lawyers, that Hinojosa guy is one of them ... he's the same one who defends those cantina killers, people who don't have a pot, 'cause that's the type of person who'll hire him for a lawyer.

Well, he got Becky to get custody of the kids. Yeah, he did. Is there justice in any of this? Tell you what, if you're looking for justice, you best wait for it in heaven, because they got none of it here in Klail City. And, yeah, the same thing happened to me with Esther. It's true.

But it must've cost the Navarretes a very pretty copper penny to pay off Judge Cantú. Sure! You can't tell me that they didn't get to Adán Cantú, got him with a bag of money, they did, and that's how Becky got the kids. Now, I ask you, how can there be justice in Klail?

What I'm about to tell you, though, is something I don't know about on a first hand basis ... But Noddy Perkins came that close to firing Jehu Malacara, again. You talk about a lack of morality, uprightness. Hmph.

And what happens? Noddy kept him. At the Bank. But I think I know why he kept him, too: it was Ira. Ira intervened for Jehu, his behalf. Can you beat that?

Me, myself, I've told Ira that there's nothing wrong with being a good person, doing a decent turn, but I've also told him not to go around wasting favors on people who can't even spell the word gratitude. 'Cause let me tell you, every person born in this world knows that Jehu Malacara is an ungracious, ungrateful lump of clay. I'm telling you he is.

All right, let's look at this: how many times, when, how many times, has Jehu ever helped the Bank during the elections? Or helped Ira

even? Not once. That's right. There's only one way to explain why
Jehu is still at the Bank ... Jehu's got, oh he's got to have, something
on Noddy Perkins. Some secrets. And that's why they hired him back
at the Klail First.

Yep, some guys are just born lucky, that's all. As for Ira, he's got
that decent streak in him, and he can't be any other way, and what can
you do?

Oh, yeah, and you know what Becky Escobar is up to now? Not
much ... a common secretary. And to Viola Barragán, of all people. So
what did going to college Up North ever do for her? Nothing, college
and all, and then to wind up working for that woman? Great Jesus ...!

I can tell you that not one single solitary day of my forty years here in
Belken County, not one, have I ever worked for or with Viola Barragán.
And here's the sign of the cross to swear on it. Other people can go work
for her if they want to. It's a free country, isn't it?

As for me, you'd have to pull a gun on me to get me to work for her.

The heat of the day drove the informant and the listener to an open
air porch facing the Gulf breeze. It's a wet, humidity- laden breeze. The
listener is served a tall glass of iced tea while the informant enters the
house in search of cigarettes.

As you know, I work for the KBC, and I'm proud to say so. Those
families know what being decent is all about. No two ways about that.

As for Viola Barragán ... she just got here the other day, as we say.
In diapers, made of discarded grocery bags, I betcha. Now, that Viola
grew up to sell herself to the highest bidder is a matter for her own
conscience to sort out. But everyone gets what's coming, and Viola's
bound to get hers someday.

I think the first false step Viola Barragán has taken in this go-round
has been to hire Becky Escobar. Take her on. That woman's going to
bring down Viola Barragán's little empire, and if you don't think so,
"wait for me on the corner, darling," as the song says. It's just a matter
of time, that's all.

I got an idea. A theory, you might say.

Noddy Perkins—no one's slicker or sharper in the world—has already started chipping away at Viola Barragán's diamond-studded crown, oh yeah. It's a theory like I said, but see what Noddy's up to: First, Jehu no longer handles the Barragán account, and I know this from the Klail Enterprise. You got to read the paper closely: Here's what it said sometime back, that Esther Bewley, Bowly Ponder's niece, has been given a new job at the Bank, and she's to handle the bigger accounts. That's Viola's, see?

Next, people who don't know what's going on, they thought Ira'd been shipped out to Jonesville, to the Savings and Loan, because Noddy doesn't want any trouble betwen Ira and Jehu. And I'll come to Jehu in a minute. Well, Ira was transferred, but here's why: Now that Noddy's got Ira Escobar at the Savings in Jonesville, the Klail First National Bank is going to start calling in its loans to Viola, and then they're going to be sold, passed on, to the Savings, and there, that old biddy's going to have to give all her eggs to one Ira Escobar himself. How does that sound?

But there's more. Just wait till I light up here ... There. Now, Noddy Perkins is going to have to retire one of these days and real soon, too. He looks tired. Okay, when he leaves, Jehu Malacara's going to be bounced out of there like a bad check. The Blanchards and the Klail family keep him on Noddy's say-so, but the first day Noddy's out of there, it's adiós, Jehu Malacara, until you're better paid. That's gospel.

The first step's already been taken: Ira is waiting in Jonesville, ready for his marching orders. I'm not saying I can see the future or anything like that, but you just think on it now. Put some of that brain power of yours to work, and you'll see I'm right; that's the play, all right. Few people in the world can measure up to Noddy Perkins, and now that he's finally seen the light, he can see Ira's merits and talent, and he's going to make full use of 'em. Not right now nor tomorrow morning, but it's only a matter of time.

And Jehu? Like I said a little while ago, that damn guy must have something on Noddy for him to keep Jehu on the job. Something big. Serious.

But Jehu'll get his too. Oh, yeah. And talk about gall, nerve, and brass ... See these two eyes of mine? Well, they've seen him with Becky, in the street, in a shop someplace. Hell, he even parks his car, the Bank's car, in front of her house. Ira's house. Like a dog marking off trees, you know ... But I tell you one thing, parking the car in front of the house and going in are two different things. That's right. The street's a public thing, you can park anywhere.

Oh yeah; there's some who've never shaken hands with Lady Shame. Look to this: Just how long did he keep the mourning for Olivia San Esteban? A weekend? Proof enough. That's a sizeable piece of hypocrisy to lug around. Sure and that's why I skip out of the Blue Bar, wherever, when I see Jehu Malacara come in. The best thing to do is to keep one's distance from people like that.

And Himself? Hmph? Comes in natural, like there's nothing to stop him ... Comes in, orders a drink, pays a round for the house and then he leaves. Show off ... Wanting to buy friends ... just how long does he think he can count on that type of friend?

If my ex, Esthercita, and I agreed on anything it was that you had to keep an eye on Jehu ... She'd say it all the time: "Watch him, Emilio. Keep your eye on him. Study him, Emilio."

She was right, you know, and I had to agree with her.

I don't know why, but Jehu has the reputation that he's a ladies' man. Bah Loney. He must be around thirty-something, thirty-eight or so, but he's never married as far as anybody knows. Not by the Church, and what judge would marry him, anyway? A ladies' man ... Where? When? Who? Well? I'm listening ... which ones?

I remember once when the Escobars first moved here. By that time, Jehu was already working at the Bank but not being able to carry his load. Just like now, eight-nine years later. Old Noddy wanted for Ira to start running the Bank, but something more important came up: County politics.

And it was here that Noddy had to come to a decision: or Ira takes full charge of the Bank as my first assistant or he can use his talent to help me with the County. Ira, and listen closely, Ira himself made the decision.

As he told me later on, and more than once, too: "I walked into Noddy's office and I said to him, 'I'd like to run the Bank and do the commission thing, too. I'm sure I can. But I can see what's going on in the Commissioners' Court, it lacks leadership, and I guess I'd better tend to that for now.' Making decisions, Emilio, is not a hard job once you make up your mind ... "

Old Ira left an out for Noddy, see? Told you he was bright ... The out was that if Noddy wanted 'im for both jobs, then he, Ira, was available. He'd run the Bank and the Court.

It's something, isn't it? To have someone loyal like that? You know, Noddy is not an emotional man, he's very Anglo in that. Not like us. But Ira's offer caught Noddy unawares, and in order not to show how much he was touched by Ira's offer, generosity even, Noddy took to coughing, like he had a fit, and that way he didn't have to explain the tears in his eyes.

Once in a while, Ira remembers that scene and he tells me about it. But the choice and decision was Noddy's, and he chose well. Ira ran for the commissioner's post, and then he was named a high officer at the

Bank.

To show you how slow some people are, there are those who say that Jehu Malacara is not interested in politics. Now, that's just not true. He wanted that commissioner's job; he even asked Noddy for it. That's right, I got this straight from Ira, and he should know.

Envy is what Jehu's got. There's a lot of raza eaten up by envy, and Jehu is one of them.

I know I talk a lot, but it's always on the side of truth, and one can't talk too much then. You got to let truth air itself out, in the sun. The hotter the better, just like cotton in midsummer.

So, when I say something, make it into a statement, it's because I know, or whoever told me knows, what he's talking about—someone like Ira, or just as good, Notary Public Polín Tapia who knows and who is in a position to know. As for Jehu, he was born lucky, and he's still riding that lucky streak. Some got it and some don't, and Jehu's one of those who's got the luck. That's right.

Born naked just like the rest of us and it's pure dumb luck he didn't starve to death. The Buenrostro family, out of pure, unadulterated charity, 'cause they're not even blood kin, you know, they raised that boy for a while. Good thing, too, otherwise he would've wound up in Huntsville State Prison, doing time.

You bet. The State would've penned him up in his teens . . .

But luck was there, waiting for him. And then he also had the luck to join the service . . . whatever else the service has got, a person can learn a lot of things there. I didn't get to go on account of this twisted leg, otherwise, I'd-a been right there, among the first.

Yeah, the Army helped that boy, and the federal government stepped in and helped him with his schooling, you know that? They had special programs for Texas Mexicans, did you know that? So they'd learn a trade, get a job somewheres, after the Army. How the federal government picked him is a mystery, but it did.

Fair's fair, and I recognize that Jehu got himself an education and all that, but he isn't half as sharp as some people say he is. Take Ira, he'd barely started at the Bank, six months, I'd say, and he was already Jehu's boss, plus being a commissioner. How 'bout that?

And Jehu'd better not mess with Becky. Oh, I know there was that nasty story, when she was still married to Ira and that Jehu this and that and so on and so forth, but that was all talk. Becky still had pride in those days. Pride, honor, and she still knew what shame was.

Now, I'm not saying she doesn't have shame now, but Jehu'd better watch it himself. He comes fooling around that house once too often and there's going to be trouble. But who's to say? Maybe they deserve each other, eh?

And will you look at the sponsorhsip? No less a personage than
doña Viola Barragán. Doña, hmph! That's some tree they chose for a
bit of shade and protection, isn't it?

If it weren't so sad, you'd want to laugh ... yeah.

contradicts previous accounts

Julia Ortegón

Julia Ortegón, piano teacher. Has known Becky from college and before primary, middle, and high school. Hair, black; eyes, very dark. Strong, beautiful hands. Wears her hair in a chongo, a bun, and held together with a gold brooch, an antique. No rouge or eye shadow here, and no lipstick either. The listener believes Julia Ortegón doesn't need artificial help. The listener is a distant relative, a pariente; their great-grandmothers were identical twins.

Well, pariente, I'll start with high school; that's when we both decided to attend the same college. We graduated together and we settled on North Texas State; music majors, the both of us.

Becky and her mom, doña Elvira, and me and my aunt, Ursula, Dad's youngest sister. You know she raised me, us, after mom died delivering Pepe, and I've got three years on him. He'll be the regular weatherman on Channel Five starting next week, instead of substituting like he's doing now.

I remember it was a weekend; took us a couple of days to get there, but I don't remember much about the trip. We did stop at Austin the first night, at a brand new motel then, on the main highway. And from there, up to Denton.

Those four years at North Texas, and we finished there fourteen years ago, seem almost like a day now. Semesters blending in and out ... And I liked Denton, it was small, something like Klail, at that time. But it was far from home, just the thing to become independent, at least for me it was.

Not too much for Becky, I don't think, though you've got to admire her now ... She's always been a very sweet person, but naive, too. It was that mother of hers, and you can't learn much when someone's on top of you, handing out advice all the time. Doña Elvira's a bit *cargante*; pushy, heavy-handed, and lacks the right touch.

My dad says she draws more water than a ship full of scrap metal. Not a bad person, at all, but she likes to order people around. As for Becky, she'd go along, but she wasn't completely broken, you know. Oh, I suppose it's like everything else.

One example ought to do it, I think. In those days, the North Texas girls would pal around with the Tessies from T.S.C.W. The Tessies'd hire buses to visit College Station, a little bit like loading cattle, it seemed to me. But that Texas State College for Women was a girls' school in those days, and they had to get out of Denton.

As for us, well, there weren't many Texas mexicanos to speak of. So, you'd wind up dating some red-faced Anglo hillbilly. Too, A & M was still a staġ college, so no coeds there. And both T.S.C.W. and A & M had a tradition of sorts: The Tessies'd go down to Bryan or the Aggies— mostly seniors, and those boots they wore—would come up on a special weekend ...

Why those Aggies didn't go to Houston, or Austin even, was beyond me. I always thought it a bit idiotic.

None of this is important, but I'm just trying to go back in time here, because that's where they met, Ira and Becky. Although both were from Jonesville, Becky came to school here in Klail, to St. Ann's, not Klail High. As for Ira, he'd been sent to finish up at Central Catholic in San Antonio after his first year or two at Jonesville High.

Central Catholic. Uniforms. A little A & M, that's all. Becky once said Ira had an ear problem ... My aunt Ursula is not a charitable person. She said the doctors had said *rear* not *ear*. And that kept him out of the real army. Not a matter of abiding interest to me, as you may imagine.

But that was Becky in those days, naive, making excuses for people, and nice to a degree. Not, a ... a ... a sly boots, okay? Just unwilling and unable to go out of her way to hurt or to slight anyone. And innocent in other ways too, and that's as good a point as any to start with, innocence.

I'd say we'd been four months into our first year there when we went across town to make our first trip to A & M with the Tessies. As far as Mexican guys were concerned, there couldn't have been over twenty-five at North Texas then. Our dates at A & M, and all this was pre-arranged, were a couple of *bolillos*—Anglos. Off the farm from the looks of them. Uncivilized would be a way to peg 'em, and so much so that they had no idea we were *raza, mexicanas*. I even spelled out my last name for them. Becky, of course, was a Caldwell on account of her

father, but she's a Navarrete on her mother's side, and that's the name
that rules in that house.

I'm as pale as a candle, but I'm a Texas Mexican, and if I ever forget
it, people in the Valley will line up to remind me who and what I am.
This too isn't important, but this is: First trip and all, this is when Becky
first met Ira. It happened just minutes before the return trip to Denton;
we were standing by the buses, waiting, when this mexicano, and wearing his uniform, struck a conversation with us. There were four of us,
talking Spanish, except for Becky. Oh, she understood every word, just
didn't speak it much, and not enough to save her soul ... those nuns at
St. Ann's were English pushers. Well, you can imagine how I got along
there those four years.

Ay, Diosito ... I knew three of those nuns, and one was my Aunt
Hermenegilda, and she spoke English the way I speak Greek, which I
don't.

Well, there we were, waiting to board the bus when Ira showed up.
I'd never seen him before, but when he introduced himself, told us who
he was, and where he was from ... I remembered my dad saying he was
a Leguizamón. Now, you and I are third or fourth cousins, right? ...
but the Buenrostros and us are much closer than that. We're Ortegón
on account of my dad, but our mom was a Rincón, and Rafe Buenrostro
and I call each other *primo* to this day.

Bells rang right away, a Leguizamón ... No, thank you, I said to
myself.

And so, there's this uniformed type who had little to offer from what
I could tell. He wasn't even homely; there was nothing there. Oh, an in-
gratiating manner, and somewhat charming—but unconvincingly so—
and what woman wants that? There was nothing else. My dad, a man
known to speak his mind in church, told me that Ira'a mind was ordinary, run of the mill. When my dad says that about anyone, that's
anyone, you may as well write that person off immediately.

I know, since childhood I've known, that my father has no love for
the Escobars or for the Leguizamóns. To his credit, he was bang center
on Ira, too.

The strange part about all this is that Becky felt the same way. Didn't
talk about him on the bus at all. She talked in that la-di-da way of hers
about Bobby Jack or Joe Ed, whatever the bolillos' names were, but
then she called home; we all did, Sunday nights, whenever. That phone
call changed her life, poor thing.

In those days getting to the Valley wasn't the easiest thing. Not from
Denton anyway. The long distance calls, then, were it, as far as visits
were concerned. An emergency was something else, of course.

Becky got on the phone first, and I was waiting in line. It wasn't anything startling. She may have said something like, "I met Ira Escobar or I saw Ira Escobar." Nothing, really. But, Holy Mary, Mother of God and all His Miracles! Everyone in line heard doña Elvira Navarrete's WHAT? Or something like HOW WAS THAT AGAIN? Why, you'd've thought the chance meet at A & M a favor from God Himself, for goodness' sake. Good Lo—ord.

What a mother! And poor Becky, is all I can say. From that moment on, doña Elvira, doña Elvira Navarrete de Caldwell, began her ... her ... her, how should I put it? ... her instructions, like speaking to a Catholic convert, can you see that?

Absolute claptrap such as how she, Becky, should behave, respond, what Becky had to do—all right, I'm using my own words here—but what Becky had to do to snare Ira. Can you imagine that type of advice? On long distance? And for such a fool as Ira? Ira Escobar? Lo—ord.

You shouldn't take all of this to mean that Becky didn't like Ira. What was happening was that she had her mother's approval, don't you see? An entirely different matter. It put a whole different color to the thing. And then, to add to all of this, to every bit of this, Ira's mother also figured highly in this ... this campaign. Oh, yes she did. You can forget what is being said now. I was there, in Denton, with Becky, and I could see those two women down in Jonesville. Yes, I could; across that distance and that time, they had a hand in it.

Becky is a beauty, I'll apologize for the word, but Becky is one. I'm not exactly a stuffed monkey, but I know beauty when I see it. Oh, I know we use the word *linda*, but she went beyond that. Still does. *Bella* is what fits her, and she with two kids of her own, too. And still a beauty, despite having to live with that fool for over a decade. But you can't have everything, and poor Becky was saddled with that mother of hers ... But don't leave Ira's mother out of it either.

Well, we couldn't make it down for Thanksgiving in those days, so we waited until the long semester break. A & M must've closed early, because by the time we got to Jonesville, Becky told me there were a dozen post cards from Ira. Mailed across town ... Oh, well ...

And? Doña Elvira was waiting for Becky in the driveway! Party invitations in hand, three parties, minimum, plus Christmas and New Year's. It had all been arranged. Like a fruit cake, everything piled on, don't you know.

My aunt Ursula and I still laugh when I remind her what she said after we dropped Becky off: "Elvira Navarrete is the world's biggest fool, with one exception: this diocese's bishop."

The bishop is my uncle Urbano, Aunt Ursula's oldest brother.

The rest of the story isn't history, it's a melodrama. Ira, and it's no secret to me, transferred from Bryan to San Antonio, to St. Mary's. He couldn't hack it there, either. It was a circus. Ira flunked out of A & M: three years, fifty hours. From there to San Antonio. And where would a good Catholic boy go? In San Antonio? But he forgot to read the college bulletin. Oh, you can make the hours at St. Mary's, all right, but you've also got to pass the comps, and those comprehensives are something else from what I hear. The upshot is that he took them and took them. A scandal, really. My cousin, Lupe Sosa, told me about it. He's the one with Valley Prudential, and he was at St. Mary's at the time.

It must've been fixed up somehow. Ira did graduate. And what's one more college graduate, right? But Becky must've known, had to. Most probably didn't think about it at all.

They married within the year after Becky's graduation. She majored in piano, as I had, but she didn't give piano and perhaps chose not to. Her home and her family, as the saying goes. *Su casa y su familia ...* Lo—ord.

All this and heaven, too. And my Aunt Ursula said little on that occasion, but what she did say was enough: "One of these fine days someone's going to tear away the cobwebs off those pretty eyes and face, and when that day comes, some people'd better watch out, they'd better get out of the way."

I guess she said it because she had known doña Elvira Navarrete since childhood, and she baptized Becky, after all. And she's known the Navarretes' history, dreams, yes, and ambitions too. Oh, my aunt Ursula knew full well and quite well whose idea that marriage was. That remark about the cobwebs? There wasn't a trace of malice in it. Not in the least. It was an assessment.

Doña Elvira is not a fool, neither is Becky, for that matter. What happens, though, is that Becky is what we call *noble*, nice, kind, malleable. You can add docile to that litany. That may come from the Caldwell side, from her dad, or maybe from the Manzano side, that grandmother of hers, nobility of character there. Principles.

As for Becky, she didn't always take the best course for her. I mean, she would defer to her mother too often. You can't do that with a bully like doña Elvira. But you've got to admit that Becky, Becky Malacara, and I wish people would stop calling her Becky Escobar ... where was ... oh, yes, Becky is a good person, *persona decente*. If there is any malice, *mala uva*, *mala leche*, as my dad says, that comes in a direct line from her mother's stark-staring blind ambition.

Too, Becky is just too loyal to her mother's wishes. And, too, she loves her mother. And of course you can ask, "Why not? Why shouldn't she? It's her mother, after all."

Well, Aunt Ursula talked about "one fine day" and that day came roaring into the Valley like one of those Gulf hurricanes.

She cut the anchor line from that ... that oaf. She then crossed her legs, as we say, and with that, she closed that entryway to Ira. The Valley, this world of ours, almost went out of its planetary orbit.

"Why, what does that girl think she's doing?"

"What's wrong with that woman?"

"Where would someone like her get ideas like that?"

No, people aren't funny. Not here. Here, they're either dumb, drunk, dangerous, or on drugs, or all three. Or is it all four? (Laughs.) No, they're not funny, and I was just quoting Father Matías Soto who, by every account, camps out at doña Elvira's or at Ira's mother's house. Ay, Dios.

The listener watched Julia Ortegón cross the living room, and yes, she too is a Valley beauty. The listener doesn't bother to ask why La Ortegón isn't married. Come to that, why isn't the listener married?

Julia Ortegón raises the thermometer a bit. The overcast sky has blocked out the September sun; the barometer is rising a bit itself, due, as Julia's own brother, the TV weatherman, says, "due to a disturbance out in the Gulf."

And doña Elvira? Now? At this point, it's best to go to an expert: Aunt Ursula. I'll go get her, but before that, how about some more coffee? Hand me that tray there.

She doesn't like this room, by the way. I'll go into the kitchen and pass on to her room. Why don't you go on out to the porch and turn that air unit on?

The listener lights still another cigarette, and, ash tray in hand, walks to the porch.

Ursula Ortegón

Ursula Ortegón. A woman in her fifties. An unmarried woman of the old school: prefers a life of chastity and its attendant corollary: independence.

Julia'll be back in a minute. She was telling me of Elvira Navarrete's fright and *choque*, the shock of it all. (Ursula Ortegón's laugh is a happy sound, not one of gloating. A sound that, to the listener, is usually the result of a particularly well-told story.)

Ursula: But I'll tell you this: such laughing will make you cry in the end, it becomes too painful to laugh. I told Elvira. Several times, too. Our friendship goes too far back to break off when harsh truths and opinions are passed on. Oh, she's touchy enough, and she's not made of wood, you know.

But, aside from Viola, I'm still the oldest friend Elvira Navarrete has. She's sloughed off dozens through the years. That's how she is, and one, I, for one, don't judge friends or parents. As the saying goes: have a set number of both and learn to recognize who they are.

Elvira is the way she is. Let us say she is sui generis, and enough said.

As for Becky, I am her godmother. My brother and I baptized her. My sister Gertrudis, she's been Sister John Birkman for thirty years, was in attendance at the baptism. Anyway, Becky, whether she knew it or not, had changed in the last three or four years of her marriage. I noticed it.

She was thinking for herself. Not much thinking going around, I'll grant you, but it was there. Let's call it a limited type of independence, and the slavery's got to end somewhere.

Nothing one could point to directly, but a little something. One felt this, and I made no secret of it to Elvira; for Elvira, you see, the world is unchanging, people become older, people die, but for her, the world keeps bumbling along ... I doubt she even reads the paper, not that the *Enterprise* or the *Courier* have anything worth reading.

I have a few strange ideas myself, but that doesn't mean that I'm a bad person or a good one. They're ideas with which I've lived all of my life: it is far better, preferable, even, not to go through a divorce. (The listener was brought up short by Ursula Ortegón, who rose and said: "Don't look at me that way. What I say has nothing to do with my beliefs or with Catholicism. I attend Mass, still go to confession, and I'm a communicant, but it's become a pastime now. Oh, I donate money, of course. It wouldn't look good for that silly goose brother of mine if I didn't give to charity. He's the bishop, after all, and that should give you a fine idea of what the Roman Apostolic has come down to. So, I believe in Mary, in her Son, and in God; nothing easier. I just don't believe in the Church. I've seen too much, heard too much in this house, in this porch, in my brother's old room ... Oh, well." Do, then, excuse the long parenthesis.

I look upon divorces as harmful, but as in everything else, I'm sure there are special cases, and Becky's must've been one of those, I suppose. But I still don't like them, and yet, as I said, I recognize that etcetera, etcetera, etcetera ... Now, that clap of thunder that rang down on Elvira Navarrete rang a little softer here, an ordinary thing, the closing of a door, say.

But for Elvira? Well! It was a moan the size of Texas and Northern Mexico put together ...

"Ursula! A divorce! Those are strange steps in our family, Ursula. We don't know the way."

Well, you would've thought the *degüello* had been ordered, no quarter, no prisoners. The Navarrete household was in mourning. Long faces. The end of the world. A bit of self dramatization, too. It's usually inevitable in those cases. But you can't help seeing the humor of it, really.

And Becky? Nothing. Did not utter half a word. And she wasn't angry, nor did she—is 'recriminate' too strong a word? Well, she didn't. Not to her mom, or to anyone. She said she'd done what she had to do, and that that was it.

But what a family! Denser than chaparral and mesquite, yes they are. And I shouldn't say "family;" I should say Elvira ... Why, you would've thought someone had died. It was exaggerated, and any type of exaggeration always makes me laugh. I didn't, of course ... I'm a friend. But a small confession is in order here: I'm no good at funerals. Some of them are the greatest exaggerations on God's Green Earth.

I know you've attended funerals in your day, and you've seen wailers and fainters and mourners who carry on and on and fall on the casket, and so on. Well, no one died. It was a divorce. And maybe that's why I dislike divorces; people can then use them to excuse almost any kind of erratic behavior. One has to set limits, exhibit some self-government ...

I told Elvira—and Becky was still there, as I said—and that accountant uncle of Becky's, the premature one, Pepe, and I said: "It's nothing, people. It's a divorce. Nothing more."

Catarino Caldwell wasn't there. Probably out fishing. Oh, and Elvira's other brother, that fool, the oldest one, Pascual, he was there too.

But I was wrong in a way. And foolish, too. In reality, there had been a tragedy of sorts. For Elvira it was the breaking of a set, a broken glass or cup. A glass of the finest, most valuable crystal. Broken, and by breaking, severing her ties with the Leguizamón family.

And you know who said all that? I'm just quoting, see? Pascual. Pascual Navarrete.

Himself, that solemn goose ... Look, Elvira has some excellent points and some weak ones. She carries ambition tatooed on her forehead, and that is her one major fault. As big as that error is, however, she is a good wife and sister, a good mother and a good friend. I'm a friend, and she and Viola have loved each other dearly for years. Viola knows her as well as I do. And ... I've sat in this chair here in *my* house, and in Elvira's favorite chair in *her* house, and, watched and listened as Elvira defended Viola Barragán, and Elvira's defended her in no uncertain terms. She will not tolerate the tiniest bit of criticism against Viola, by anyone. Elvira has this idee fixe regarding the Leguizamóns, but Elvira is loyal, *leal y noble, no-ble.* Her family has been in the Valley a good many years, but the Leguizamóns have become a special project for her.

She's got too much Navarrete blood for her own good. Had she had a tad more Manzano blood, Elvira would've been one of the happiest women of her generation. Believe me. Listen, God knows exactly what He's up to: Who did Elvira marry? Answer: Catarino Caldwell. Second question: Who does Catarino resemble ... in character? Answer: his mother-in-law, doña Leola Manzano, Elvira's mother. But it's that Navarrete bloodline. Believe me. Oh yes, the blood does need tempering now and, then.

All right, who does Becky resemble? Her father: a jovial man, a bit aloof, but kindly. Sometimes serious, and above all, peaceful, one of God's own, as we say, and a die-hard enemy to ambition in any form.

This is not my description, although I agree with it. This is Elvira talking and how she's always described him.

And Catarino Caldwell himself? Nothing. Quiet, pleasant, and when he does talk it's to say where he's going, and one always knows where he's going and his destination, too: fishing or hunting. Except for Elvira and Becky, there are no other women in his life. He's not a smoker or a drinker nor a skirt chaser.

He adores Becky, spoils the grandchildren, and Charlie loves to fish with his grandpa.

And where does Ira stand with his father-in-law? Catarino is courteous. But then, Catarino is that way with everyone. Now, if his daughter, who is worth both of Catarino's eyes to him, and his heart, too, if Becky is happy with Ira, fine. But if his daughter has now chosen to divorce her husband? That, too, is fine. That his daughter now says that her life with Ira is unbearable, then she has to be believed, because his daughter, Becky Caldwell, is not a liar. And there you have it.

On the Navarrete side? No need to go on ... Becky did not divorce the late President Kennedy or anything close to that. The divorce is Elvira's via crucis. She had placed every hope, all her eggs, as it were, in that bridal basket.

You'd think this was stuff of the nineteenth-century, the union of two families, and so on. Ira Escobar is an ordinary boy. Common. Run of the mill. A normality among normalities.

Let's look at him. Nose? I don't even know what size it is. Eyes? Brown? Dark? I couldn't tell you. Hair? It's either curly or it's straight, but don't go by what I say. Manners? Good, I imagine. But then, every Valley boy I've known has 'em. So?

Oh, here's Julia now. And with fresh bread, too.

(Laughs.) Do you know what Julia says about Ira? She says that Ira has no distinguishing features, that he's not even homely enough to comment on.

He is one of God's unfortunate ones. If he had ears like a bat, say ... something, but he hasn't got a thing that'll set him off from the crowd, poor thing. Oh, he's got a bit of the Leguizamón jaw, but that's about it.

All I can say is that he may be a bit of a bore, and if he is, then there's no cure, no redemption or salvation. There can't be, in God's own world, something worse than a boy who, as a man, becomes a lethal bore ... It's best to drown them early and young, like cats ...

Coffee and hot rolls. Buttered pastry. The listener lights a cigarette.

And Elvira? That very afternoon. You can just imagine. She came here at a gallop. Drove straight from Jonesville. She forgot about the phone, and she loves the phone. It was about this time now. Julia here was on her way to the garage when the screen door, that one there, let in a rush of air, a cyclone. Elvira! Panting. Gasping. Her eyes out of focus, looking in all directions, seeing absolutely nothing, her voice rising ...

Becky, Becky, Becky ...

My first thought? Oh, Dear God, killed in a car wreck. I dropped whatever it was I was holding and I went to her.

Water. Limeade. *Vino tinto*. Something, and then that voice again, and: Becky, oh Becky ... what have you done?

Julia missed this part. She was in the garage looking for something, but even out there, she could hear Elvira. Well, Julia rushed in expecting holy murder at the very least. (She turns to Julia who nods.)

And to top it, Elvira wouldn't settle down, and we couldn't get her to sit and tell us. A gasp, a pant, and: BeckyBeckyBecky ...

Well! This had to stop. We sat down and waited her out amidst her tears and hiccups, don't you know. And then, she told us, but I'll tell you what set Elvira off and running ... it was Becky's look of determination, resolution: One of those, "This is it, I'm not moving, and you go ahead and do what you want to."

Elvira could have saved much of her breath on that one. As for that Pascual Navarrete, that other brother, I'd've taken him with that cricket voice of his, and thrown him in the nearest lion's cage, let me tell you. He's a cloying piece of little manhood. A lap dog in a man's suit is what he is. And tiresome? He's like a barnacle on a wreck ... Good Lo—ord.

But as I said, it was Becky's irrevocable decision, that's what Elvira saw. And, it frightened her. Resolution pure and simple, if it ever is that. And you know what else she saw in Becky's face? Elvira saw herself, and she saw Becky had had it with Ira. There was no going back. Elvira could see that Becky had considered the decision coldly, *fríamente*, and seriously.

Poor Elvira. Couldn't recognize her own daughter. Couldn't see that Becky, in spite of everything, was a person, a human being. Someone with character. Someone apart from her little daughter of eight or nine.

Becky and Julia here have known each other for years and Julia's

always said that Becky, as pliable as she's been through the years, did
have certain limits, limits which once crossed ... mmmm, then it was
lookout! Yes.

Oh, I can imagine how much Becky must've cried alone, yes, alone,
and thinking of the scandal, of her mom, and thinking of her own life
with Ira ... a life she now found unbearable. Can you imagine all of
that? Oh, yes. Becky has had to put up with Ira, and that's a tall order
... Once, about eight years ago, she paid me a visit, alone. That was
eight years ago, and she sat right there, where you're sitting, and said she
was in love with Jehu, and Jehu loved her ... (Julia Ortegón is aghast.
She can't believe her aunt who continues speaking.

And why shouldn't she come to me? I'm her *madrina*, I baptized
her, and she lives, what? ... a block away? Anyway, she came here and
sat on that same chair.

I made a gesture of some sort, said maybe she was wrong. That she
had two kids to care for, had reached a certain age, and that perhaps,
just perhaps, someone can come and pay attention to her, and that she
thought she was in love. Hm. Becky, quietly, said she wasn't "in love,"
she said she loved him.

I remember quite well. She didn't cry. Not a tear. She took my hand
and in that moment, she looked like a señora, a senora who will always
know more about everything in the world than I will ever learn or hope
to know ...

"You're wrong, madrina." And that's all she said.

May Julia here forgive me, but there are some things, certain things
one can't share, can't pass along. Can't tell anyone. It's not important
now, but perhaps this may clear up some things. I just don't know anymore.

The reader may know what silence is, but with three people in a
room, sixty seconds of silence seem longer, somehow. Ursula Ortegón
placed her coffee cup lightly, measuring every millimeter, or so it seemed
to the listener.

As for that Malacara boy, I confess ignorance. Adopted, perhaps, but blood kin to the Buenrostros. I do know Mati Buenrostro looked upon him, treated him, too, as she did Rafe, and the other two boys. I just don't know him. Oh, I see him at the Bank. At a function once in a while ... but know him? No. One hears things ...

A kind, relaxed, and knowing look, and then:

But Becky knows what he's made of. And I can imagine how Elvira could see herself in her only daughter's eyes. And painfully, too, for poor-dear-foolish Elvira for whom the Leguizamón union represented the sum total of her life. Dear, merciful God, what a goal to aspire to ... And it was that exactly, a goal.

Sadder still, though, was that that was not the sum total of Becky's life. To live to be thirty-odd yearsfor one's mother is to give her another thirty years of life. That's not doing anyone a favor of any kind ...

The children? Charlie and Sarah? I don't know. I don't know. One never does know. I never thought of being a mother, and I raised Julia here. And I know she loves me (smiling, finally), despite my secret ... but a secret, any secret, no more makes than breaks a love, friendship, respect.

At this point, Julia rose to turn on the six o'clock news. Her brother reported that the hurricane had settled or stalled some two-hundred miles East Southeast off Jonesville. He then gave the coordinates and said: "That's all for now. Back to you, Bill."

Julia laughed at this and explained that what we were watching was this morning's tape spliced to the six o'clock news. Julia laughed again and said it was merely another form of reality.

The listener helped with the tidying up and noticed, perhaps mistakenly, that Ursula Ortegón looked older, somehow.

Martín San Esteban

Martín San Esteban. Pharmacist, two years older than his sister, the late Olivia San Esteban. The listener has nothing else to say about M.S.E. at this time.

Jehu and I did not get along when we were kids. I think we get along now. We speak. Too, we don't see each other very much. We run in different circles, that's all.

We were up in Austin together. And I didn't know whether he first didn't like me or whether I didn't like him. There must have been some sort of, ah, antipathy. That happens, doesn't it?

Around that time, the war in Korea was either over or winding down, and he was fresh out of the service. Jehu and his cousin, Rafe Buen-rostro, showed up in Austin and registered at the University. There were very few of us Mexicans there at the time, and most of us were from the Valley, some from Laredo, El Paso, San Antonio. Not many though. There were also two other cousins of Rafe's there, Raúl San-toscoy and Cheo Campoy; they were in pharmacy with me. I had a roommate from El Paso, and he too was in pharmacy.

We all hit the beer joints pretty regularly, especially on weekends. In the Fall, during football season, that was a sure thing.

It was a strange thing between Jehu and me. We never talked about it, we didn't then, and still haven't, to any great degree . . .

I doubt if the rest of the guys ever even found out, 'cause Jehu and I never came to words, let alone a fight . . . It was strange. Of course, if Jehu ever said anything to anyone about himself, or how he felt, it would've been to his cousin, but as I say, who's to know? Besides that,

76

who was ever going to get a word out of Rafe Buenrostro, right?

What I do know is that Jehu didn't date my sister Livvie up there, probably never even danced with her at the Newman. We were damned few raza there, and so, one turned to *bolillas*, the Anglo girls.

Our dad's family, the San Estebans, we're not related to anyone in the Valley, that we know of. My mom and dad came from Querétaro, just like the Buenrostros, but my folks came here in their twenties, during the Mexican Revolution ... They got here yesterday, as they say in the Valley. We, my sis and I, were born on this side of the River, first born sons of foreign-born parents.

There were three of us: Merced who was four years older than me and who drowned in Campacuás Lake during a picnic on the lake when a blue norther rolled in. Took everyone by surprise ... The month of March ... and then, just like that, the norther was on us, wind, cold wind, and hard rain, driving rain ... Livvie's death ... well, that took place a little more than two years ago. I think about her everyday. It was Livvie who got me to change my mind about Jehu. He was single for years after the university, and he ran around; maybe that's not the term. It may be unfair, too. He knew a lot of girls ...

Me, I got married to San Juanita about a year after graduation. That was the expected thing then: education, marriage, a family. It certainly worked out for San Juanita and me. I've no complaints, and especially when I look around ...

So, Jehu's teaching at Klail High, quits, and from one day to the next, it turns out he's a banker. First, he worked at Klail Savings and Loan and then, from there, right across the street, and kitty corner from here, the Klail First National Bank. It was Jehu, in fact, who managed the loan, the loans, really, for this place, and for the pharmacy my dad, my sis, and I opened up in Ruffing.

Jehu signed every copy of the contract very carefully, neatly, not carelessly at all. He smiled when he was signing and he said to my dad, "Don Salvador, this'll teach 'em a lesson." My dad laughed too. It was like a joke between them, see?

As I recall, Livvie wasn't at the Bank. She was checking at the County Clerk's and at the title abstract company one more time.

Later on I found out why she checked so carefully. Jehu had called her on that. He told my dad, and made it a point, too, that sometimes, somehow, titles are made to disappear, changed. Anything, he said, anything can happen at the County Clerk's office.

Too, Livvie later told me, we were to be the first Mexican-owned pharmacy in the Anglo part of Ruffing ... But somebody had to go in there first; and my dad, he'd chosen a good location, a sound location, and Jehu had sent a loan appraiser to take a measure of the traffic, the parking, the marketing end of it. All business and you sure can't say that Jehu doesn't know what he's doing. Livvie's checking off all the property titles and surveying was part of Jehu's careful checking on everything. A businessman's way ...

He and my dad have always gotten along. When Jehu stopped his running around, his fooling around, some four or five years ago, well— I can tell you when exactly—it was the time he came back to the Bank for the second time. At any rate, he called on my folks, formally. Set a date with them, said what it was about, and he was there in a week or so. Formal, see? He and Livvie had already agreed on this, too. My parents, both of 'em, were touched by this, impressed that Jehu made it a point of formalizing it ... ah ...

Oh, they knew Jehu, of course, what with business and all. But he called for an appointment, *una cita*, as I said. He showed up and that was it. It was very nineteenth-century, you know? 'Cause, shoot, here in the Valley now, one asks the girl and then she *tells* her folks what *she* plans to do. I mean, Jehu and Livvie dated, and he was serious ...

And it wasn't until then ... What I mean to say is that it wasn't until then that I could see that Jehu wasn't what I thought he was. What no one thought he was. Hmph. One time back I'd gotten angry as hell, I should say resentful, because Jehu wanted Livvie to go to med school. Yeah. Up in Galveston. I was wrong. Flat out wrong. It took me a long time, but I finally saw that I, who always thought of myself as someone on the ball, you know what I mean by that? Well, I was wrong, about a lot of things. I wanted Livvie to stay where she was, what she was, a registered pharmacist.

And Jehu? Nineteenth-century ways in some ways, he wanted Livvie to be something, to study medicine, go up in the world ... I guess you first have to learn to read people ...

I can swear to anyone that Livvie was never happier in her life than in those two years in med school. And Jehu? Waiting for her. That's why he came back to the Bank the second time. He had the Ph.D. to study for, but he said that was of no consequence, no importance ...

He lied. I know he lied. If he dreamt of anything, it was to return to Austin, Texas. Oh, yeah. But he came back to Klail. He and Livvie broke off for a while, but they made up. I don't think there was ever any doubt about those two. Jehu laughed about it at the house one day; he said that lovers falling in love again always happened in bad novels.

As for me, I had to admit something that was very, very difficult for me. But I had to admit it: Jehu didn't care whether I lived or died, truly. If I was surly at him, or if I resented him and his ways, it was all the same to Jehu. The resentment, and I had to own up, came from me. I didn't like him. I didn't like his ways or the person.

And Jehu? None of this bothered him. He sure didn't show it at any rate. And then, when he fell in love with my sister, he fell in love.

Whether I or ten-thousand other guys were going to be the brother-in-law didn't bother, didn't concern him in the least. He only had eyes for her. Me and my parents, other people, dead, as far as he was concerned. The one time I saw anger flash in his eyes, briefly, but enough to see the fire, he said, "Goddammit, Martín," like that, in Spanish, "You've got to think of other people." A strange guy. So I changed. I realized he wasn't a bad guy, not self-centered at all, just dead serious. And strange, yeah, strange.

So now, marrying Becky, well, that doesn't surprise me. He's serious, just like with Livvie. Jehu's not here to change the world, he takes people and the world without ... ah ... say ... ah ... preconceived notions. Right?

Took me some time to learn that much. My folks were happy when he married Becky ... I didn't even know they'd heard of her.

As for Ira? He's all right, we get along well ... but look at it honestly: Jehu didn't break up that marriage. He didn't take Ira's wife away from him. He didn't insult him, show him up. That's not Jehu, that's not his style. Oh, I've heard, been told, that Jehu and Becky had something going eight, nine years ago. I don't know that. It could have happened, though. He ran around a lot ...

As for *this*, now? This is Becky's own doing. She is a divorced woman, a working woman. She's free to do, undo ... She gives no cause for talk that I know of, and if she and Jehu reached an agreement, married, 'cause they are that, well, they're both well over twenty-one years of age.

As far as any of this concerns me, Jehu Malacara is not about to ask my permission for anything. He was faithful to Livvie, kind, considerate, and even though my sister's death was the most painful thing I've gone through, Jehu behaved as if they'd been married.

Look, it's easy to look the fool in those cases, but Jehu showed class, demonstrated it, without wanting to or without any pretension whatsoever. And what matters most, above all, and everything else, to my folks and to my wife and me, is Jehu's sincerity. No room for hypocrisy, no, not in quiet actions there isn't. He cared. Very much.

I had no idea when we started talking here what I'd say. I certainly didn't plan anything. But I must say I never thought I'd be talking about Jehu in this or in any way. But Jehu showed us, me among them, by example, that it's best not to say, "I'll drink not from that fountain."

Yes. The way things are, the way some people are ... and yet, we're still not close. But there's respect now, and we share that. Yeah, I think we do; and that's the way it should be.

The listener has some ideas and opinions to express. The Valley is a strange place, to begin with. The speakers that follow—Valleyites to the core—are at home, at ease, both in English *and* in Spanish. They are all Texas Anglos, and they are all bicultural, to use an old term now used popularly.

There are Valley Anglos who claim they are bilingual, but aren't. It takes work to speak as a native Spanish-speaker. Then, there are also those Anglos who say they wish they were bicultural and thus bilingual, but they're neither. This also takes time. And there are those who were born to it; it had nothing to do with work, or wanting to or wishing for it. They were at home, at ease.

As the listener insists, it's a strange place.

E. B. Cooke

E. B. Cooke. 1) A Williams College alumnus and graduate; 2) a graduate of the Harvard School of Business.

As far as I'm concerned, and from where I sit, it's live and let live, I always say. What better way is there to ensure domestic peace and tranquility?

I was born in the Valley, in February, 1910, and as many of my class, my military class, 1910, that means I learned Spanish from day one. Ranch Spanish, obviously. In college, at Williams, I spent my summers in Spain, Havana, Mexico, and so on. I'm saying this not as a brag, not entirely, but only to clear up any misconception. I'm Valley-born and I know the *gringada* just as intimately as I know *la raza*.

Well now, since I can hear and see and know the difference between right and wrong, to live and let, as I said, I don't think that Becky Escobar's leaving, abandoning, divorcing Ira is bad or good. A matter of complete indifference to me.

Regarding Ira's political career, it must be on its fifth or sixth year or term, whatever, but that's nothing to me either. Boys like Ira are in long supply and there's even more now than there were ten, twelve years ago, let's say. As for Ira, I'd say he was competent in a narrow, restrictive way.

Too, today's Becky Escobar—and I say this privately and publicly, since it doesn't matter to me, anyway—Becky is a different proposition, not the same Becky at all. At all. And I like her more, too. She's ... she's her own person, know what I'm saying here?

Oh, she's always been nice, pleasant, tractable, let's say, but when

I look at her, I see some bearing, some direction. Carriage, that's the
word I was looking for ... Sure of herself, too. Who she is, that she's
aware of that, see?

If at one time she sat—and will you listen to me talk this way?—if at
one time she worshipped at my niece Sammie Jo's feet, they now treat
each other as equals, something which Sammie Jo likes, by the way. My
niece, as Churchill used to say of Russia, is a paradox wrapped inside
an etcetera ... So what I'm saying is that Sammie Jo hated—despised,
really—the way Becky, the old Becky, would abase, would efface, erase
even, her own character to go around pleasing other people. And this
to please those leeches in the Music Club.[2]

Well, as for Sammie Jo, she prefers for people to be themselves, not
the way other people would like for them to be. You do understand
that, don't you?

The listener is not hard of hearing. Informant Cooke's tic is not to be
taken as a penchant for corroboration, in any way or case. The listener
believes that these *huhs*, *rights*, etc. are breathing spaces as Cooke goes
from topic to topic. A manner of speech tied, it is obvious to the listener,
to Cooke's character and personality. Indifference, then, to everything
but his own person. In this way, not different from most egoists.

As for Sammie Jo, she's loved one man in her life, young Rafe Buenrostro. And who would've thought they'd ever marry? No one. Not
here. In the Valley.

Her sad, unhappy life has been due to her father's idea of improving
on an empire. That brother-in-law of mine ... and no, it isn't an indis-

[2]The deponent's first and only wife left him for a Brazilian, perhaps an Italian, tenor.
E.B.C. has consistently laid the blame on the Music Club.

cretion if I speak of Noddy this way. I started it, so I'll end it here. But let's get back to Becky.

Becky, and here, above all, frankness must be brutal, home truths, then: Becky's gotten hold of an elm tree of a woman friend and protector in Viola Barragán. And even if Becky neither knows nor appreciates it yet, she's a young Viola Barragán. A seedling, let's say. She's sharp, handsome, honest, and as one must be in business, tough. She's got the future in her hands, she does. What I'm saying is not some cliché or other, these aren't set phrases; make no mistake on that score.

But aside from all this, that future that I ... that I presage, don't you know, is being claimed here with all the confidence of one who has known, dealt with Becky at first hand. That first year after her divorce, she'd go with Viola to all the businesses in Viola's corporation.

And here we are, halfway through the second year, and what do we see? Well, there's Becky administering various of the business enterprises: the hamburger chain, the Shopping Bags, that massive trailer park which, by all accounts, holds some nine-hundred place units ...

With that number of trailers I've already told you about, more or less indirectly, Viola's investment in that venture is substantial. You see, the average range of those mobile homes goes from nine to eleven-five when bought in those large lots. That is a very serious amount of money. And Becky? She's the one who rules that little-wheeled kingdom. The café chain, and there's eleven of those, that's a rift of gold right there. Oh, yes. You see, Viola, with Becky's advice, has added chicken and a salad, etcetera. The Shopping Bags are frosting on the cake, let us say.

And as I just said, Becky is the director of those businesses. I'd bet dollars to doughnuts that Ira couldn't carry that load ... *no puede con los liachos*, eh? Talent's the trick, and drive, too, knowing your personnel, to show, receive common courtesies, tact ... That's necessary; did I say necessary? Essential is the word. Well, Ira's not the one, hasn't got the knack, the talent. He's got other things going for him, and you can't deny that, but he's missing that little something, *el toque*, that Becky's developed to a high degree. Learned that from Viola. Either that, or she was born to administrate—a gift.

The change, maybe it's best not to call it that. The discovery of her own persona, who she was, as a person, well, that opened up the floodgates, the whole dam, really. And it had to be opened in order to fulfill its mission, carry out its assignment ...

The listener, attentive as ever, suspects that E.B.C. has gone off the track here. Slightly, but off. The listener has full confidence in the reader and knows the reader will get the drift.

The children? Fine, as far as I know. The oldest, a boy, is no longer enrolled at St. John's. Becky placed him in public school. The girl's no longer at Scholastics either. She's at St. Ann's, here in Klail. Becky's old school ...

Socially, I imagine I see her and Jehu once a month, the old *rendimiento de cuentas* ... the settling of accounts payable and receivable. It's business, but social, too.

As for Jehu, he and I've always respected each other, and that is not only a truth, it is a completely verifiable fact. If Noddy Perkins and I agree on anything, and there isn't much to hang on to, both Noddy and I recognize Jehu's talents and contributions. As Jehu says, though, praise is a great thing, but a raise is even better.

And as I said to you over the phone, I was a witness to their wedding. Jehu himself asked me to serve.

A seventy-two-year-old witness ought to count for something, don't you think? (E.B.C.'s laughter).

Yes, Jehu is well-paid, and why shouldn't he be? By the way, Jehu took himself out of Viola's accounts, a valued account, too. Jehu said it would be improper. So, he himself went out to the main office, picked out Esther Bewley and trained her for the job. That's Esther's office, across the hall, personal office and everything as associate director of current accounts.

Jehu's been named cashier, my old job. I just come in here for coffee, something to do ... This old office used to be the board room. I heard Jehu's name here for the first time; he was at the Savings and Loan then ... As far as the Bank, as far as I'm concerned, as one of the owners, what Jehu did in withdrawing from Viola Barragán's accounts is enough to inspire confidence in anyone. Shows you how he's grown as a banker and as a person. That's right, as a person.

Hmmm. I remember my sister Fredericka, who's no longer with us, how she resisted Jehu's hiring. It wasn't Jehu, it was the idea of what he was ...

Jehu would've made a fine lawyer, just like that non-practicing cousin of his ... my nephew now, right? In-law, but a nephew ... Anyway, Jehu's grown. He asked, first me and then Noddy, if it wouldn't be bet-

ter if he were transferred to Klail Savings or to our branch in Jonesville
... soon after the Escobars' divorce ... Well, about a week later, the
three of us met in Noddy's office, a Friday, if I'm not mistaken ... end
of the week, end of the quarter ... Anyway, Noddy mixed some high-
balls and after this and that, Noddy broached the subject of the transfer
and said, "No, I don't want you to go out there."

Said that Jehu would stay put—you know Noddy—and that he'd
talked to me—he had—and that he'd phoned Junior Klail and I don't
know who else, maybe my sister Anna Faye too; that we had agreed he
was to stay at the Bank.

Years back we knew he was a Buenrostro, and here we were, the
Cookes, about to hire him ... Well, there are only two Cookes left now,
Anna Faye and I, since Freddie died of uterine cancer. Freddie came
around though, although if anyone has ever been born a Mexican-hater,
if there is such a thing as being born that way, Fredericka certainly was.
Once, just once, Jehu and I talked on this, and Jehu attributed Freddie's
... her discomfort with Mexicans, as good, old-fashioned guilt. Talking
to me that way, about my own sister, but then I had brought the subject
up in the first place ... And he wasn't being flippant either; he also said
it didn't matter, that the land, this land, the Valley, all of this, would be
here when we were all dead. He then laughed and said, "When the state
has withered away." Noddy it was who christened Jehu as The Uncommon Banker ... he is that, all right.

Since we do get on, although just barely when he was first hired, I've
learned that I'll get an honest answer; cool, perhaps, but an honest one.
One day, out of the blue—well, perhaps he'd considered it deeply, but
out of the blue for me—he said that Ira needed an eighteen-year-old
girl. You know, someone around that age, without character. Terrible
thing to say, but there it is ...

Edith Timmens

The listener is sitting on the east-side porch of a so-called ranch style house in South Klail City. Enclosed and air-conditioned usually, the glassed louvers have been opened widely, and the strong Gulf breeze cools the shaded porch after a driving rain earlier that morning. According to the latest weather reports, hurricane Elmer remains a hundred miles off shore, lurking, and continues to be a threat to the Valley and Northern Mexico.

The frosted pitcher of limeade looks inviting, and the listener pours two tall glasses, adding a sprig of hierba buena, mint. The second glass is intended for the listener's hostess, Edith Timmens, widow of Ben Timmens, attorney cum public relations drum beater cum one-time state and national congressman for the KBC interests.

Edith Timmens née Bayliss is Valley-born. Strong, resolute, and with a mouth where butter doesn't stand a chance. Discreet at times, outspoken at others, the listener has always found Edith Timmens to lean toward the truth, although it must also be admitted that euphemisms and circumlocutions may be employed when the informant deals with her own family. The KBC and its families, however, are presented as she, Edith Timmens, sees them. Not a gossip then, but she has heard and participated in too many of the KBC lives and doings for her to have to succumb to niceties and shadings in this regard.

My Ben never did learn Spanish, astonishing as that may be. Couldn't get the hang of it, he claimed. A poor head for languages was another of his excuses. I never, for one minute, believed him.

He didn't want to, and that was plain enough to me. You can lie to almost anyone and get away with it, but you can't lie to your wife. Not convincingly, at any rate. Oh, she'll go along, pretend to believe, perhaps, but taken in? No, that's not the same thing. For his part, his lying about why he didn't learn Spanish was stupid, but Ben was also a bit of a racist. And don't look at that admission as a betrayal of his memory or as the lack of loyalty of a widow. Ben was a racist, and he had little reason and no excuse for it. His mother was Mexican, and one who didn't speak English, and how do you like that?

The Timmens came here by way of San Luis Potosí. Ben's great-grandfather served in the Confederacy. He married into a Southern family which had settled in San Luis after the Civil War. Ben was brought here this century by his father, Big Ben Timmens, the one who married a Mexican from Potosí. At that time, my father was the chief KBC veterinarian for the Klail Division of the Ranch, the Atticus Klail *potrero*. And, it was he who saw to it that Big Ben was made a *caporal* right off. That's right, foreman of the K Division ... His wife was named Petra Cedillo, and she died of dysentery when my Ben was eleven or so. About the time of the Spanish influenza epidemic of 1919 or so. Anyway, Big Ben then married Laura Pennington when my Ben was thirteen. Laura was his mother. He called her that, and she reared him, cared for him, but that didn't make her his blood mother, *su mamá*.

And speaking of my father, now there was a piece of work. Raised on cactus milk, as we say. Not originally from here, but he might as well have been born here. This was home, he said. Virginia? That was just a place to be born in. As for Spanish, not once did he insist we learn it or that we had to, we just did. Never a question of if or when. Made use of the maids who raised us, of course ... simple as that.

I was raised as a KBC-er, and my Ben was too. The KBC paid for our schooling, all of it, Austin, Georgetown Law, wherever we chose.

I loved Austin, Washington, too. Happy years in Washington, but I'm a Texan, through and through. And don't take this talk of mine as a smokescreen to hide anything about my brother Hap. He was always a delicate child. I'm no psychiatrist, and I can't begin to tell you why he turned out the way he did, but he did, and I'm not here to whitewash anything or anyone. I'm already a hypocrite in my own eyes, so I certainly don't need to cover up for anyone. Every family has its own rarities, and happily, for us, Hap knew how to be discreet. He didn't accost anyone in a man's bathroom in some restaurant or library, and he didn't approach any young accordion players or whatever ... You and I know what I mean, and that's the end of that.

As for the KBC, they're sharp as red pepper, but they're odd, too. To my mind, they've never enjoyed their money. Have never known how to and that's a sad truth, a truth as big as Texas, as big as the Ranch.

They lack something; a taste for life in some strange way. And they're skinflintish, too. In a phrase: they've not been able to find pleasure in each other as a family. I'm not talking of one or two nor will I spew out names for you, but as a whole, an unhappy bunch. And you can forget about taste. Everyone took a separate road there, although the roads all lead to the same point. And Klail City itself? The town would've died if it hadn't been for enterprising Mexicans and Anglos, believe me. The KBC wanted an enclave and discouraged whatever looked like growth ... But this was a Mexican town, had been since the 1700s ... The Valley's history is no secret, after all.

And I'm not opening any old sores here; that sore is very much alive, and the KBC knows it. And they're lucky, and smart, at the same time ... They've made huge blunders, but they've been written off ... my Ben saw to that many times.

Of all of them, I prefer Noddy and Sammie Jo, and their company and friendship. They laugh, smile, and they're a pleasure to be with. And Noddy's wife, Blanche? The very devil herself, and I mean that in a nice way: she's a wit. And she drinks, and she knows it. She doesn't lie to herself.

Sammie Jo? Adored by both of them. They're a lively damned bunch and both mother and daughter love and suffer together, and who wouldn't? After all, living with Noddy wouldn't make for one continuous barrel of fun and laughter, would it? Still, the three are a team. As for Noddy marrying off Sammie Jo, a crime. Two, really, since he pushed her into two horrible disasters ... And Sammie Jo? She understands her father's weaknesses and insecurities. Do you actually believe it is easy to marry into the KBC?

As for Blanche's drinking, it was a serious problem and remains so. I'm not here to defend her, even as a friend. Alcoholism is not to be defended or excused, you've got to admit it, your friends have to admit it, everyone. Blanche is much better, and I think seeing Sammie Jo happy has helped her. But let's not blame Noddy Perkins for Blanche's drinking. That's the easy way out.

As for Noddy, red-faced, that irritating nasal twang, and that cool, chilling side of his at times—all of that, when it comes to his wife and daughter he is the picture of consideration and sensivity. He knew he was wrong when he engineered those weddings ... And now? Some people laugh and say Noddy is stuck for a third time, and this time with a Mexican for a son-in-law ... The only thing cheaper than talk is people's bad breath, and I would suggest they save it and their saliva, too.

I go on like this because when my Ben was down with pancreatic cancer the Perkinses were the only ones from the KBC who came to visit him. Noddy, most of all, and Sammie Jo and Blanche would send flowers every other day. They would do the arranging, too. And Noddy was there, in the room. I knew we were friends and we visited, but this is Mexican *cumplir*, isn't it? ... *ser cumplidor* ... I once heard your cousin Jehu say that about Noddy ... It wasn't until my Ben fell ill that the true meaning of the word came to me ... Hit me full-face. And E.B.? Not once. Not ever. Anna Faye. Not her.

Poor Ben, was he ever wrong about who'd stand by him, and he was even wrong about Becky Escobar ...

The listener was offered several drinking choices: iced-tea, iced-coffee, or limeade. The listener was also offered a cigarette from a box of Delicados. The listener chose limeade and a Delicado as did Edith Timmens.

No doubt about it, my Ben was a fine lawyer, and always well-prepared, too. But he lacked the human touch; he worked for the KBC all of his professional life, and he never represented anyone else in court. Not that Ben spent much time in court, anyway.

My father, years ago, had passed on some sound advice to me: don't you ever fall in love with institutions of any kind. He said it to Ben, too. My father knew full well who he worked for and he wanted Ben to understand. I understood. Perfectly. Poor Ben, he was loyal and he expected loyalty. Good thing he didn't ask for it. He loved the KBC, lived for it. And he a lawyer ...

And here I was, protected by this Ranch and its power, having to remind myself of what my father said, and having to remind myself that the KBC did put the food on the table and the clothing on my back ... But also remembering that this wasn't charity, that work was performed, that the food and clothing were earned, not given. One has time to think in a hospital. One can only read so much ... And Ben, Ben was in pain, and so I cried for both of us.

The day before he died, Jehu Malacara walked in. After shaking hands with me, he walked to Ben and shook his. It wasn't much, his only visit, but it set me to thinking of the first time I saw him at the Bank years ago. I didn't like what I saw; I was frightened, I think. He carried about him a whiff of independence, something the KBC considers dangerous. "He won't last," I remembered thinking.

Just a whiff of it, but enough to recognize it. I had been independent when I was his age, perhaps. Later, when I saw him, and I was in my fifties then, I also understood there was a difference between that kid—Jehu—and me. And between him and Ira, too, later on. Sammie Jo was a big help in this case. She once said that Jehu was prepared to leave the bank at any time; nothing to it, he'd told her.

Oh, yes. He hadn't fallen in love with the institution. And? ... Well, he did leave. Oh, he came back, but it took three years, and when he came back, the look of independence was still there. Not a defiant look, that one used by people who feel inferior and who adopt a pose or something. Not that at all. A self-assurance, a nice way with people. Warm, courteous. The way he behaved with Ben at the hospital, with me.

No, he wasn't about to go under the way Ben did and the way Ira did when he came on board ... Ira sank, disappeared without a trace, didn't he? Who is Ira? is a fair question.

I've seen and talked with him since the divorce, since Jehu married Becky. Ira has yet to see, to understand the connection between Becky's disaffection, the divorce, and the direction their life had taken, was being led.

As for Becky, she finally met a man who loved her, one who knew how to love, to care. Jehu needs no instructions from me, he can distinguish between a person and an institution, to get back to that again. But it was true, Jehu saw her as a person, as an individual, as a woman full-blown and grown. And Becky had changed, oh yes ...

And it happened, one afternoon, about a year after the divorce, Jehu—and this comes from Becky—Jehu called on the phone. Thirty minutes later they sat on the front porch overlooking Klail Boulevard. In the daytime, nothing to hide. A chat, brief, to the purpose. I can only imagine what was said— Becky didn't go into that—but it's common knowledge from that day on Jehu called on her and they went out. Nothing secretive about that.

That Ira was subsequently transferred to Jonesville gave people a lot to talk about, but Noddy told me, in person and as a friend, that it was he who had Ira transferred ... His decision to make, with the KBC agreeing, of course. And Noddy doesn't run away from decisions. But here's the clincher: If Noddy hadn't acted on it, then Ibby Cooke would have. That's right, E.B. himself, even if not for the same reasons as Noddy. But do let's get one thing straight up here: Ira is still very useful to the KBC in county politics. Too, it could well be that Ira likes that kind of life. Takes all kinds, as you know. Life still smiles on him, as Ira sees it; some of that "it was great to be alive, but to be young was really heaven." That's Ira all over. Well, Becky wasn't getting any younger. Now you see?

A break. The postman comes by to the porch door needing Edith Timmens's signature. The listener, meanwhile, takes a walk around the living room. No expert on furniture as to period or style, the listener does recognize fine workmanship: wooden pegs, hand carving, old brocade which looks better with age. The listener also counted six cigarette ash trays; nothing fancy, merely serviceable.

Where were we? Oh, yes. Well, the last time I talked with Becky was last year sometime. She was leaving the Camelot, we said hello and talked without sitting down. Less than a minute, I'd say. And then, and I couldn't tell you why, but I reached out and gave her a peck. She grinned at me. You know, I truly believe she knew what the kiss was for. Funny. A slight raise of the hand, the slightest tilt of the head. She said it all without saying a word.

We talked about a lunch date, but you know how that goes. I keep up with her through Sammie Jo; they see a lot of each other.

And Sammie Jo? Forty, last month, and every time I see her, I remember the day she was born. I was there, at Klail General ... Blanche Perkins almost died giving birth and it took her over a year to recover. Her health even before the birth was never the best. But there was Blanche, sickly, weak, nursing her and she did so for more than a year. Blanche's own life hasn't been the healthiest either in every sense. But we're the way God and the world and life itself fashions us. Blanche is special, what Rafe Buenrostro calls *una persona*, right?

And as for Sammie Jo, well! Headstrong and wild as a kid, and then those two horrible marriages that ... Well, the past belongs to the past and that's what cemeteries are for, anyway. She's always loved Rafe. The opposition at seventeen was formidable: the whole of the KBC, and Noddy, and I, oh yes, and her so-called friends, and Mexicans and Anglos alike. But if you live long enough ... right?

Beyond that, a long life is useless unless you grab happiness by the throat and hang on to it. Sammie Jo did; Rafe was happiness for her, and she never let go; not even when he married soon after high school, before the Army and all that ...

Oh, I know everything about Rafe going to the Bank and all that followed. Yes, and Sammie Jo going to live in the house El Quieto built years ago. I would've given both eyes to be able to've gotten inside Noddy's mind when Rafe walked in, even with an appointment, which he had requested ... A tough, tough rock, that Rafe.

And that too is what Becky saw in Jehu: a rock, one which wouldn't crack; a diamond, one which couldn't be bought, could never wear out ... Someone in whom Becky could confide, say things to. Something. Anything. Life!

Becky. I saw myself in her years ago, in that little climber, as she was then. A trimmer of sails for any occasion, one who wanted all of everything. Until she learned that what she was going after was what her mother wanted ... had wanted all along. Poor Elvira Navarrete, and poor Edith Timmens, too, who also wanted it all ...

No, not a matter of luck, of drawing lots ... Becky merely found a second mother, Viola Barragán. And if Viola was not the *madrina*, the sponsor, when Becky was born, that was due to Elvira Navarrete's weakness, poor thing.

Viola Barragán remained her friend. For life, in it for the long pull, as friends must be, are. Viola has not only seen a great part of the world, she also knows the world. Why do you think she and Noddy get on so well? Ha, they've both taken this world on its terms and reached the same conclusions. It's there, take it, oh yes, but don't fall in love with it, don't be surprised by anything that's in it ... I got mine from books, which is a silly way to live. But not those two, not Viola, not Noddy ...

Viola had a hand in Jehu and Becky getting together, but it wasn't her doing. Jehu, who can zip up his own pants, thank you, went to Becky. This new Becky I'm talking about, this Becky who has the intelligence to see things clearly, who saw in Jehu what she needed to see. He went to her, but only because she couldn't come to him. And who knows? The new Becky would have gone to him in time.

It's called love. And that's all there is, but it's enough, isn't it?

And now, what do you say to lunch? On me ... well (laughs) ... on the KBC.

Bowly Ponder

The informant Bowly Ponder is a police officer assigned to the Belken County Sheriff's Office. A native of Klail City, and uncle to the just mentioned Esther Bewley, the bank administrator. Ponder, although the listener has no direct knowledge, is said to be in one of Noddy Perkins's hip pockets.

If the listener had been given to choose one, and only one word to describe the informant, the chosen word would be elliptical.

I know Rafe Buenrostro much better than I know his cousin Jehu Malacara. But it also happens that I got to know Ira Escobar through Jehu himself. It was all a big coincidence. It happened that Noddy Perkins had sent for me, to the Bank, not to the Ranch; you see, around that time, I was still on patrol here in Klail.

Noddy needed my help, he wanted me to help out in a couple of things dealing with the county elections. And since these were not city elections, I had no conflict of ... ah ... ah ... no ... ah ... conflict of interests according to lawyer Ben Timmens. Aside from that, to render some sort of service to Mr. Perkins is only right, smart, and proper ... One should always take the opportunity.

Mr. Perkins and I were talking about what he needed me for when Jehu Malacara walked right into Mr. Perkins's office, no knocking or anything. I remember he nodded at me, and I also remember, and quite clearly, too, that Noddy Perkins didn't act surprised. He didn't introduce us either. I knew who Jehu Malacara was, of course. My niece Esther Bewley was Jehu's secretary at the time, and she always spoke well of him. And too, the way Esther talked of him and of Ira Escobar, you could tell right off who was her favorite.

But to tell the truth here, Ira and I have always gotten along well. Real well. He treats me with respect, consideration, and I've always been ready to help him in anyway. And why not admit it, right?

Both of them, Ira and Jehu, work for Noddy, and as for me, I've said it twenty times over that Noddy Perkins has always been one of my strongest supporters. Always, and I'm proud to say it.

Ira Escobar, I'm sure, will say the same. He's still the County Commissioner, and one needs all the friends one can get.

So ... given my current post with the County Patrol, you might say I've also had the opportunity to know Ira's wife, Becky Caldwell. And I know the kids, too. They usually ride around with their mother, and it's obvious she's a good mother ... As far as the separation business and the divorce, that's their business, and I see no reason why I should cut through that briar patch ...

Too ... ah, and how big is Belken County anyway, right? As a County police officer, I get to know about people's lives. Part of the job. One sees and knows things ... No need for me to explain, is there?

And things being the way they are, and they are that way ... Well, I can assure you that Becky Escobar is not mixed up in drugs or in smuggling of any kind. She is a businesswoman, and there's her office to prove it in that company owned by Viola Barragán.

Don't take what I've just said to mean that Becky Caldwell, ah, Escobar, I mean, Malacara now, right? It's not to be taken to mean that she's been under surveillance. What happened was that Ira Escobar had once asked me to look out for her, for her well-being, but that was it. They hadn't gone through the divorce at that time, see? ... and he, Ira, just wanted to be sure that Becky was all right, that no one would come by to pester her, you know. A precaution on his part, that's what it was.

I didn't see then, nor now, anything wrong with doing a friend a favor. They're divorced now, and since Becky got custody of Charlie and Sarah, Ira again asked me to look out for them. A continuation of the favor, let's say. Being divorced, of course, doesn't mean that Ira is going to abandon her ... the kids ... I mean you have ... you know. And Ira's a man of morals, ethics, and as he's explained it to me, he wouldn't want for someone to come and dirty up his name, or Becky's either. And he was also looking out for the ki—-the children, too, as I said ...

And ... ah ... we ... ah ... and things have now changed somewhat. I mean, well, Becky has remarried, hasn't she? And this, of course, has put or puts, rather, a different color on things, to be sure. I mean, her life, the one she leads, is respectable, right?

It also happens that ... that Mr. Perkins had called me in some days ago that there'd been some sort of complaint ... Not against me, not that. But a sort of complaint from someone who ... that Becky was bothered, ah, didn't want to see a car, or county cars ... parked by her house, you know? Or patrolling ...

This was a favor to Ira, right? And Mr. Perkins let me know that he, ah, understood perfectly ... Why this arrangement ... And that County Patrol cars could be put to better use elsewhere. And I agreed ... As he said ...

And it's now been a while that my niece Esther Bewley, told her mom, my sister Sally, that Ira'd been transferred to Jonesville. Esther said this for a purpose. Oh, yes. She told her mom to let me know about the transfer ... let me tell you, I didn't like the way Esther said it, but those are Mr. Perkins's orders, so that puts another light on the subject. Know what I mean? But it's Esther's way of putting things ... She said, "And Mom, tell Uncle Bowly to lay off. He'll understand what I mean." That's how she put it.

I, ah, I couldn't've said it any clearer myself ... So I called my brother Dempsey and told him to let the Commissioner know of the new arrangement.

As I said just now, I agree with Mr. Perkins, although I was also very careful to point out to him that I was just doing Ira a favor, nothing more.

For his part, Mr. Perkins said he understood perfectly well I was just rendering a favor, but as he then pointed out, there was no further need for the patrol car. He went on to point out that Becky was a married woman and, as such, did not need, ah ... require is what he said, did not require County protection. Yes ...

And as I've just been saying, I agree with Mr. Perkins one-hundred per cent. Well, that's where we were when Jehu came into the office and nodded to me, like I said. I ... ah ... I tried to read his face, maybe some sort of something, like a gesture, you know? He and Mr. Perkins talked for a minute or so, then both of them signed a whole bunch of papers and in the middle of the signing, Mr. Perkins he let out a big laugh and then went back to signing. But don't ask me what that was all about.

Not two minutes later, my niece Esther pops in and Mr. Perkins got up, said "thanks" to me and handed me a Cuban cigar. And I left, got out of there. An hour later, a call is patched through while I'm driving around. It's my niece Esther, and she says Mr. Perkins was very happy, very satisfied with the way I carried out my official duties. And like I say, Mr. Perkins is a considerate man, and one ought to be helpful and considerate right back, isn't that the truth?

Lucas Barrón

Lucas Barrón, aka Dirty. Bar owner and thirty-third degree Mason, (York) and uncle to the listener. Corpulent, as we say in Spanish, congenitally red-faced, in his mid-sixties and, to quote him, "No, not quite as strong as an ox, anymore, but more intelligent, at this stage." The listener was baptized at Our Lady of Mercy Church by the informant and by the woman who shared everything with him for over forty years of marriage, the listener's aunt: Doña Socorro. The informant, and not as a by the way, is a staunch supporter to Jehu Malacara.

Friends, you say? Which ones? Look here, you're old enough to know better: friends disappear, they die off, they move on and away, and as sometimes happens, they're no longer friends. You sure you got all that? And if you're talking about those women, forget it. For-get-it.

Listen, Becky knew those women in those clubs, but did she have friends there? No. Friends are something else. I happen to think that it's difficult for a woman to have men friends and I certainly think it's hard for certain women to form strong friendships with other women. There are exceptions to everything, got to be. Hell, what kind of a world would this be without exceptions?

But those women, those clubby types, they may have been friends to each other, but the question remains: where was Becky in all of this? Where did she fit in? Mexican girls have other problems ...

Ha! Listen, that one of our girls, *una chica nuestra*, wants to go to college, to a university, what usually happens? First off, who and what does she think she is? She must be one of those who don't like men. What kind of a father, a mother, allows a daughter to go off, away from

96

the Valley? They'll say she's crazy, some screw loose somewhere. How many times have I heard people say that? In this bar? Jesus . . .

No, I admit it isn't as bad as all that now, today, Thank God, but even today, right now, you can still hear it. God, yes. There's a lot of ass-holish *raza*, out there. Oh, and wait a minute, let me add that she damn well better not try to be anything else other than a grade-school teacher. She better not go earn a living at the Klail-Enterprise as a reporter or at the Jonesville Courier or something like that. A piss ant teacher, you slut, 'cause that's where you belong . . . Sure. And some of their own brothers say that. Maybe not slut or whore, but it's the idea. So, too often, even if just once, too, some women will never forgive other women. Why, they're just like men, yeah. Sure, it's sad, but it's the damned truth, too.

Oh, and you know what they also say? It's because we were raised that way, to think that way. Well, that's not the whole damned truth, no sireee. In Becky's case it was an entirely different matter, and that was the best stroke of luck ever. An only daughter, somewhat well-off by Valley standards, and since her mother, Elvira Navarrete, was a bit pushy, it was she who saw to it that Becky went off to college. To get married up there . . .

Enough to make you stop drinking . . . But what a drubbing Elvira took on that one. Becky wised up a bit, didn't she? Oh, sure she married, was almost forced to. The usual, you know . . . Although, in her case, she was married off to a perfect idiot. She married that son of Angustias Leyva and Nemesio Escobar. Poor quality semen on both sides, and that's for starters.

That marriage was nothing, you understand? Nothing special. A common, ordinary marriage: money was spent, pictures taken and posed for all over the place, newspaper stories, and from there, to raise a family. Like I said, common, everyday. But then, not only common and every day, it was sad, too.

But look at how things stand now. That drop of water falls hard and steady, long enough, that rock's gonna crack eventually. Got to. And in this case, the divorce had nothing to do with money, or the lack of it, no. Not at all. Nothing on that account. Becky sharpened up, and she got the living scare of her life to see herself at her age anchored to that Fat Zero. Jesus . . .

And remember the pharmacist, Olivia San Esteban? Applies to medical school? Why, even her own brother, Martín, yeah . . . bad-mouthed her, and maybe not directly, but to be sure, he was against the idea. What a crock! But typical, typical.

And you remember Socorro Tuero? Named for your aunt . . . What did she do? Studied to be a vet, graduated from Up North, and God

Almighty, she almost starved to death here, in the Valley, 'cause those jackasses didn't know what to do with a woman who could treat cows and horses. Poor kid left the Valley at a hundred-miles an hour. Had to. Moved Up North. Houston, some place. Took Socorro some twelve damned years to get back here. Toughened her up, too.

Made her better than tough, 'cause toughness wears out with time. Made her independent, and that's harder to get rid of than live-in in-laws. God, yes. Impossible. Okay, say she'd've stayed here? What then? Oh, sure: go to work for the KBC. She'd done that, she would've sunk like a shrimper in a hurricane ... Gone, and to the bottom, too. Became, made herself independent. And that's exactly what Olivia San Esteban wanted to do.

No, no doubt about it. This Valley of ours can be a pure-dee-mean sonofabitch, like your Dad used to say. Remember? And the Valley's unforgiving, too. And forget the Anglos on that score; the *raza* itself can stick it to you like a choya cactus patch.

All right, try this one: there's Angela Vielma; she lives with Rafe Buenrostro's sister-in-law. What do you say to that? Angela has talent, brains, and she's no stranger to party politics. She's been a lawyer, for what? Ten years? Fifteen?

And she's a Vielma, all right: high forehead, eyes darker than the ace of spades, and a good, loyal, smile. And she paid for her own education, too. That was a hard-working family, and money didn't rain down on them. The U.S. Army money for Pepe Vielma's death in Korea was something Angela didn't touch. That's right. She didn't think the money was dirty, no. She just thought the money should go to her mom and dad. That's what Angela is made of.

Well, it took her longer to finish than most, but when she made herself a lawyer up at Austin, the Vielmas gave her the money from the Army insurance. They'd saved it. That's what Pepito Vielma would have done, they said.

Did you know that your cousin Jehu was over there? Jehu Malacara once told me that his cousin Rafe was right there when Pepe Vielma died in Korea. Artillery fire, according to Jehu. This is some country we live, isn't it? Jesus.

So ... don Prudencio Vielma and his wife had saved the insurance money, and that's how Angela got her start. About five years after Angela had been practicing the law and living with her folks, she bought herself a house and that's when Rafe's sister-in-law moved in.

Ha! Did those two give enough reasons for people to talk? But the talk didn't last long. Two unmarried women, oh, yes, and people who'll talk on anything and for no reason, well, they talked. Opened fire on them, they did. Then they got bored. Jesus ...

First of all, whose business was it? Bunch-a-goddam snoops, that's what. Put-your-nose-up-somebody's-ass type of people, that's who. Got nothing better to do.

Well, the very same damn thing happened in Becky's case when she drop-kicked that damfool Ira Escobar. Right away: it was this, that, the same old crap. Why, to hear people talk, a stranger to the Valley would think we were a population of saints here. Jesus ...

And then, Becky went to work for Viola Barragán. To earn a living, for Christ's sake. And let me ask you this: Who the hell's business was that? What did people want, anyway? Did they want her to stay at home all day long? Was that it? Well, they're crazy as hell is all I got to say. She's a doer, she's educated ... she's active. Is it crime to earn a living, dammit?

And what about Viola and her business? Drugs? Smuggling? Viola is tough in business, and so am I, 'cause there's no second place in the business. That's right. And this too is the truth: Viola's got a couple of things up her sleeve: she's honest, and she'll drive the hardest bargain ever, but her checks don't bounce. And when it comes to *honradez*, honor, I'll stick by her up until the day someone can prove she's otherwise. Up to that time, my word stands.

I've known Viola's father since the '20s, when they got here, one hand in front and one in back, as we say. That's all they could call their own. Telésforo Barragán, without one word of English in his head, without knowing even one person in all of Klail, he came here with his wife, Felícitas Surís de Barragán, and Viola, a baby in her father's arms ... And to work, goddammit.

Telésforo kept books and accounts, he taught at the Mexican schools we built, and he farmed, too. And he worked in the worst job there is: uprooting mesquite trees. Try that for exercise ... Whatever there was, there he'd go. The thing to do was to work, to bring food home. And how did Viola come out from all that? Ha!

You and I are related, we're family; so, family aside, I'm willing to beat the living shit out of any mortal who says, dare says it, I swear, a single, solitary word against the Barragáns. If Viola hired Becky it was based on Becky's talents, and that's a freezing fact. Oh, she'd've kept Becky out of friendship to Elvira, but without responsibilities ... that kind of thing. We all do that, to help somebody out ... But she earns her keep, she does.

Now here, in this *cantina* of mine, people talk, and that's why God invented *cantinas*. That some double-barreled jackass like Emilio Tamez comes and says what he says, or some C.P.A., some Certified Political Asshole like Polín Tapia comes here and talks, that's okay, too. A place is a place and your uncle runs a bar here, not a church.

But there's a limit, you can't cross a certain line, and all of us know it when we reach drinking age in a *cantina*. That line gets crossed, and I take over. That's why I own this place, by God.

They want to bad mouth Jehu, and they do so, that's one thing. But for them to say it to Jehu's face, that's something different. No sir. Something like that can cause a fight in here. Jehu's got an education, but he won't run.

But why worry? There's no more than two balls hanging between Tapia and Tamez; they wouldn't dare ...

As for Jehu, he'll put up with a lot, but let's face it, he's not Jesus Christ. I mean, he doesn't have all the patience in the world. So, those who talk can go right ahead, but they got to remember what they're in for ...

Jehu doesn't give a damn if someone says something about him. They just better not say it to his face. Think about that. He has a very good idea of who he is and gossip or rumor are just that and nothing more to him. But, as I said, people better not get the idea that he's going to spend his life crossing and uncrossing his arms. That he won't act. Oh, no. The biggest water tower in the world gets filled up and spills over, and that's a big truth.

Let me put it this other way, why do you think that neither Emilio Tamez nor Polín Tapia come in here when Jehu's at the bar or having a beer in that booth there? Or look to this: Why do they settle up, pay, and get the hell out when he comes in? Well? I said they were assholes, I didn't say they were fools.

If they were fools, they'd be picking some of their teeth off the sawdust, 'cause that's where they'd land after Jehu got through with them. Jehu likes a good joke, and he'll put up with a bunch-a-shit just like anybody else, but there is a limit.

Now that he's married, he won't fight, I mean, he's got to set an example for Becky's kids, his kids ... It doesn't look right, does it? Made himself into a man, that boy. Fearless, and that's the frightening kind ...

You don't know this story. Once, and Jehu was just a kid of eleven or twelve, no more than that, he killed a rabid dog. By himself. Went out in the middle of Klail Boulevard, a .22 in hand, and bam! A little later, but this you do know, when the late Baldemar Cordero killed Ernesto Tamez? It happened right here, in my place. This place. Well, right there, not two feet from that table there.

Around that time, Jehu was working at his uncle Andrés's gaming house. And Andrés used to rent the back of my place here, and that's where the gambling took place, right by that unpaved alley back there.

Young Cordero knifed Neto Tamez, but after long provocation and to hell with what Judge Phelps said then or says now. Right here, look. See? Neto Tamez fell right there, and he fell screaming like a new born. A minute or two later, here comes Jehu by the back way with a bag full of money he'd carried over from the gaming house and told me to keep it for his Uncle Andy.

Jehu didn't say a word then ... He saw Balde, knife in hand, who was walking toward the door, and then Jehu threw a glance at Ernesto Tamez.

It's too goddam bad to be a kid and to have to see that kind-a shit, but he didn't say a word, like I said. He looked at me for a while and then a few seconds later he lifted the bag and said: "Dirty, here's a bag of money from Uncle Andy."

You beat that? Tough little piece-a shit ... But he's been like that ever since he was a kid. A good kid, too, and so much so that when don Manuel Guzmán went for him to don Celso Villalón's ranch ... what? You didn't know this? Well, he did; Manuel went to pick up Jehu at the goat ranch so he'd register in school, and Jehu lived with don Manuel and doña Josefa for some time. He sure did. Manuel, in peace now resting, used to burst out laughing when he'd talk about it. He'd say: "That so-and-so will never be president of this country 'cause he's a *mexicano*, but he sure as hell isn't going to die of hunger either. Not him. He ever gets an education in him, people would do well to bet on him. There's some good blood there."

And Manuel was right, wasn't he? And now, Jehu married to Becky Escobar, well, not Escobar anymore, she's a Malacara now. One of us ... And Jehu did get a little money when don Víctor Peláez died years back, two-hundred dollars, a gold watch with fob, and a Stetson.

I took the money and straight into the bank during the four years of high school, Jehu's army service, and then four years up at the University. The money grew some, not much; I then borrowed money against it, and bought him two lots with it. As Jehu says, "I work at the Bank so I can keep my eye on the money Dirty put there in my name." He's a good *cabrón* ...

But Jehu's always been respectful, and helpful, but he won't come up to you walking with his hat in his hand. He's very Malacara ... My father, you know, got to know Jehu's great-great-grand-father, don Braulio Tapia. Balls? Like a bull's, a man among men and the poorest of the poor. *Hombría*, manliness. All of the Malacaras have been fine husbands with one exception, my compadre Andrés Malacara who was a chaser. Jehu chased, too, but he was single. But, when they settle down, they settle down, and they won't set eyes on another woman.

Yes. He did the right thing in marrying Becky Navarrete—Caldwell. Jehu will know how to be a good father to Becky's children. You'll see.

Becky *es persona* according to Viola Barragán and Viola's not the type to go around throwing away money, words, or compliments. And she knows what she's talking about.

This bar and the two lots on either side and the one across the street, the one Urban Renewal came and leveled all to Hell ... all of that property belonged to me. It belongs to Viola now. And the day I die, the I.R.S. is going to get Ned-shit from me. Damned people've diddled me enough during my lifetime ... Sure. Becky took care of the paper work. Ha! Leave it to Becky is what Viola said. How about that? That damfool Escobar had no idea who he'd married. No idea. Damfool thought he was riding some broken-down mare ... Wrong as always, that boy.

Now. When I die, it's adiós to the Aquí me Quedo. This *cantina*, which I owned and operated in four, five places in town, but always with the same name, will die and the name with it, when I die. That's right. Just as soon as Ramón Rosales loads me up on one of his hearses, Viola's going to put up a big brick building on all three lots. An old folks home. Air conditioning. Heat. Lights. Three or four floors or more, whatever the money I'm leaving gives for that. A well-made building is what Viola wants. Brick, not no goddam hollow cement crap. Brick, and with air conditioning, like I said. And heat. Yeah.

It's a good idea, and people will live with dignity, *con dignidad*. Oh, I know there's some Anglos who stick their old folks in homes, and shoot, some Anglo folk in Klail don't even know where their kids live. But the Anglos will live there, too. They're going to live in my monument, 'cause that's what Becky calls it. So those old Anglos, abandoned some of them, are going to have to live with *la raza* under the same roof. That, too, is Becky's idea. She's got some idea, she has ...

Well, I say it's time for a Buddy Watson. What? No, no, it's still my bar, and in my bar, I pay; family or not. Well, is a Budweiser okay or do you like Ess-litz?

After the one beer, my uncle Lucas went behind the counter and pulled several Closed notices; he passed two of them for me to hang outside of the Aquí me Quedo cantina: Closed. Death in the Family.

After this, Lucas Barrón took the listener by the elbow, out the door, and to dinner.

Otila Macías Rosales

Otila Macías Rosales. Wife to Alfredo Ramón Rosales, owner of Morales Funerales, "At Your Service." Otila stands four-feet ten to the listener's five-nine. Otila does not wear heels, an affectation, she says. She never has, and assures the listener that she, Otila, does not suffer "the short person syndrome." The listener understands all of this perfectly well. The listener and Otila graduated from Klail High eighteen years ago.

Good to see you! (She laughs) Mrs. Rosales, at your service, and married these fifteen years. (More laughter) Macías, as you know, on my father's side. Old don Cayetano, known to all as don Tano, the Tight-Rope Walker, and Morales on my mother's side. She was the daughter of the famous third baseman, Down Town Morales, who was the best infielder Klail City has ever produced. I'm also a Parás, on my mother's side, and she, then, was a younger sister to don Orfalindo Buitureyra y Parás, pharmacist and propietor of The Herb Shop, El Porvenir. What they now call a *Botánica* ... We are from Klail, Klail-ites or Klail-ilians. Just like you. I heard you been going around talking to people, and I thought I'd give you the family facts, ha!

You may not know that my uncle don Orfalindo, despite his age, knew Jehu very well, and closer when Jehu first went to work at the Bank. Bright, well-educated, is how my uncle described him. And he would say that drunk or sober, and that is saying something.

It is well-known, as Reverend Mora says, all of us as God's children are as fragile pieces of crystal. It is also well-known, I say, that my uncle used to go off on some serious *parrandas*; those drinking bouts were long and prolonged. Why, his fame and theirs, the *parrandas*, covered all of Belken County, extending to Dellis County. This is hardly something to brag about, but then there's no reason to deny an incontrovertible fact, is there? I don't put on airs about anything, and my husband, Alfredo Ramón, always says this about me. We're fragile, and my late uncle don Orfalindo stood at the head of the line.

My Alfredo Ramón, born and raised in Flora, where the hardy people come from, as he says, hired, some while back, a *sepulturero*, a burier, that some people called Ecce Homo. Did you ever hear of him? That isn't his name, you understand. His name is Damián Lucero.

Well, now, this Damián was a farm hand from Up River, and he worked as a gravedigger, like I said, a burier, but he could also embalm, if called upon. He's still alive, and he's older than the Holy Mother Church of Rome ... As old as he is, he works at the same bank Jehu Malacara works, the Bank.

Ecce Homo is a man of discretion, judgment, and also a man of few words. He says he owes his job to Jehu. Jehu, though, says and tells him otherwise. Jehu says that Damián Lucero works at the Bank because he's a good mechanic and that's why he's paid. I happen to know that Ecce Homo was a friend of Jehu's father, out in Relámpago, and that's a truth the size of a whale.

And I can tell you this, too. Ecce Homo buried Jehu's parents, first the mother, then the father, and Ecce Homo groomed and watered the two small plots for years. And for free. That's the truth.

After a lifetime of work here and there, and in and out of the farm fields, Ecce, I mean Damián ... Damián did not have enough quarters for Social Security. So now, with his job in Noddy Perkins's bank, Damián Lucero receives his social security, and he works, too. I swear that I am not the smartest person in Klail, but I think I can see Jehu's hand in all of this. Back when you and I were kids, there was a line in a *tango* by Gardel which ran, " ... si precisás un amigo ... ," if you should need a helping hand ...

So let me tell you, that Jehu Malacara married that divorced girl is a good thing, a great thing. My husband says she's a fine person, despite the divorce, and why shouldn't she be, right? Is a divorce the worst thing that can happen to a woman? You can forget that. There are worse things in life, many-many worse things. My husband Alfredo Ramón also says she works for a living, and is employed by doña Viola, that she went to college like you, and that she's nice, and that people say she is.

As far as I'm concerned, all of that, to me, is as fine a recommendation as you can get. On that account, and from what one hears and sees, the divorce matter means absolutely nothing. If the Church has a worry, let the Church worry about it, if it wants to. Better yet, the Church's priests who come to the Valley, should come prepared to speak Spanish, YESSIR. I say this with some heat, because once in too many whiles they'll send us some Irishman or a French guy, and worst of all, one of the damned Spaniards whose tongues, I swear on St. Elmo, Patron Saint of Sailors, I swear those Spaniards have tongues that just don't seem to fit in their mouths. So they send that type, old Church, old Church, old Church. Irish, French, Spaniards, whatever. Divorce is bad, yes, it is terrible, but it is also human, isn't it? I mean, animals don't divorce ... so what do they recommend? Prayer and reconciliation. That's what comes from not being married, don't you think? *Que recen ellos, nosotros a trabajar.* That's what my father used to say: Let them pray, as for us, we got to work ...

Anyway ... who understands those *gachupines*? I bet even they don't understand each other. As for the French, well! And the Irish? They can say what they wish, but that's not English, is it?

May God forgive me, but I only go to Mass to go. I lost my religion along the way, and I like what Jehu said one day when he brought Damián Lucero for a visit.

"All you have to do is believe, have faith. Everything else, what they demand, that has nothing to do with believing."

How about that? That's the type of advice I can live with.

My Alfredo Ramón says Jehu is right. I do too, and that's why I think that he must be something special. Got to be.

He's firm; *firme.* He's there at baptisms, marriages, and burials. He knows a lot of people, and they know him back. And now that he's married, his wife's kids go out with him from time to time.

I was raised in the old-fashioned way, and I think that people who come through in a pinch are special people. When my uncle don Orfalindo passed on some two years ago, Viola Barragán and Jehu attended the funeral and brought wreaths, flowers, and I'm talking about fresh-cut flowers, none of that paper stuff or those plastic ones, either.

Of course, everybody in the world knew that my uncle was madly in love with Viola, but one of those far-away loves, nothing to it. A theoretical love, you know? It was one-sided, and yet Viola, not once, laughed or said a word. That would've hurt my uncle. Oh, I know he was a sad, ridiculous figure and all that, and who knows? Maybe in his old age he began to believe that he had poisoned Viola's first husband on purpose ... He didn't; he was an apprentice pharmacist at the time, and he had no business concocting anything for anybody ...

You know, he would've died of happiness had he known that Viola had come to his funeral, but that water has gone out to the Gulf and back since that time.

As you know, my husband and I work together. Not in the body business, but in tailoring. I'm a tailor. A tailoress? Whatever; I design, cut and sew dresses, blouses, all kinds of skirts, and I can fix up coats and such. I can do anything. And, because of the tailoring, that's how I came to know Becky Malacara. And I also got to know her tastes, her preferences.

She knows material, too. Knows what it's all about. Cashmere this, or Indian wool that, or cotton, Egyptian and Pima, she knows. Better than that, she knows what she wants. First class in clothes. Buys only what's necessary, not a waster but not a haggler, either. Judges quality, can distinguish. And she knows how to treat a person.

As for shoes, well, I don't know the first or the last thing, and that's the truth. She does. And as I said, when it comes to quality goods, she knows what that's about. Well, when she sent that shrimp trawler called the Ira Escobar to the bottom of the boat basin, and then turned around and married Jehu, that should've shown that she was no fool.

And listen to this: Her mother, doña Elvira, for years, has come by car, from Jonesville, so I can fit her up. Her tastes are somewhat exotic, know what I mean? I was learning the trade then; you remember doña Elenita? Now there was a seamstress ... Anyway, Becky would show up with her mom, and she must've picked up her knowledge then.

There's some raza in the Valley with more money and time, but they lack the *mesura* ... the touch and feel. Why, not even Sammie Jo can beat her, and that red-head's no cow, right?

Take silk. It's a delicate fabric. A treacherous piece of material, and Becky can wear it. That comes from knowing what goes with a body ... she's something like doña Viola, who can wear a box suit better than anyone I know or have seen on the television.

The listener had heard, from other sources, that Becky Malacara was a spendthrift. Otila Macías Rosales's words give the lie to that report. What the informant also stated, "Her children dress nicely, but not tailor-mades; that's silly," is also revelatory.

Reina Campoy

Reina Campoy (baptismal font name: María de los Reyes), the oldest woman, Mexican or Anglo, in the whole of the Valley, from the westernmost parts of Dellis County to Belken County's eastern reaches on the Mexican Gulf. The Campoys came to the northern bank of the Rio Grande, this part of Texas also called Nuevo Santander (originally Nueva, with an *a*, Santander), in 1749, with the Escandón colonists. Reina's great grandmother, doña Mauricia Puig was born a Spanish subject in 1814; at age ten she was a Mexican citizen; by the summer of 1836, she was a Texan. Later, in 1845, an American when Texas was annexed that December 21st; *aquel día, 21 de diciembre*, as the the old *corrido* says.

A citizen of the Confederacy in the 1860s, and an American citizen again after being duly Reconstructed to the lights and likes of General Sherman. Doña Mauricia's son, Jaume (and that is Jaume with a *u* and not Jaime with an *i*) fought for the Union in the 1860s.

Jaume's sister, Montserrat, married the first Rafael Buenrostro in the Campacuás Mission in the mid 1870s. (Reina, who does not like the appellation doña—an idiosyncrasy—is a memorialist.)

That piece of noise that a woman marries more than once carries no weight with me; it isn't a novelty, in other words. I've buried three husbands, and the second one wasn't even my husband because I had divorced him, and that was years before I married Julio César Campoy. But! To leave a man, to abandon and desert him, and then to tell him to-get-the-hell-out, that is something special, very special.

At my age, it's hard to pull any kind of surprise on me. Nothing surprises me anymore; from the assassination of President McKinley when I was a child, to that bomb in Japan, or that some time ago an Anglo from Up North made himself into a capon so he could be a woman from one day to the next . . . Nothing. I'm old, I'm over ninety years of age, and if I've learned anything in the Valley, it's that there are people around this world who are capable of anything. *Sí, señor, sí,* as the kids say.

And Valley people are like that, too. Valley people can work hard, get drunk, and they can die in France like my first husband, leaving me a widow at twenty-eight. That's right: we've got people for everything in this place.

That the one and only daughter of Elvira Navarrete sent Young Escobar on his way—*lo mandó de paseo,* right?—well, all I can say is Good For Her. That she remarried, that's just dandy, too. Life's no better than a widowed bitch-dog. Life won't forgive or forget; you'll die anyhow and it's a fool who deserves to die with his face to the bedroom wall.

Is this too fast for you? Here's what I mean:

My father was born in 1860, and he was thirty when I was born, and then he died thirty years later on account of the Spanish influenza, something you certainly never knew about, *a Dios gracias.*

Now. When I became a widow in 1918, my father said something like this: See here, María de los Reyes, this damned country has already buried one husband, and now you're thinking of marrying a Pulido. As far as I'm concerned, Odón Pulido isn't worth the price of one cumin seed; two, tops. But that's up to you. You're a grown woman once married.

But, I'm still your father, and I'm saying this because I know how much you're worth. You've got good blood in you, mine and Santoscoy blood on your mother's side. The Santoscoys live for centuries, and you will too. So, you decide, María de los Reyes, if you marry, and you live a long time, is it to be with Odón Pulido? You're what? Thirty something? Okay. Will you put yourself underground with that Odón Pulido? The world's got more than its quota of shiftless, idling sons-of-bitches, you know.

My dad was right. Well, when my brother-in-law Macedonio Campoy first came around here from out Toluca Ranch way, he came with one purpose in mind: to marry me. I was married to Odón at the time, you follow?

Macedonio proposed to me, in person. Right in my face, as we say. And, as I said, me a married woman . . . Right then, right there.

Well! Poor Odón Pulido shrugged his shoulders, and adios, *Reina de mi vida.* But he was a good man, Odón, and years later Macedonio and I went to his funeral by Media Luna lake. A nice, clear day ...

Panic? Gossip? Noise? All and more, and then what happened? What usually happens: people conveniently forgot what they said ... My family? They said it was no one's business. Now, I had no brothers, and given the way things were then, maybe that was a good thing. But my father ruled, and chances are he would've told them not to be damned fools. Odón and I divorced through the Court House in Klail. Mace and I married here, in Relámpago.

To live and to learn is what people say ... Well, Elvira Navarrete came running in here two years ago, hiccuping and mewling and puling and saying, "What will people say ... the family" and every foolish thing she could think of in that holey head of hers.

I put a stop to that. "Sit," I said.

I then lighted two cigarettes and handed her one of them making sure the lit part faced me, given her state of mind ... After this, a jigger of mezcal with anise seed, some of that unleavened bread I'd made that morning, and I always add anise to that too. Anise is healthy for you, you know.

I was the first person in God's own Rio Grande Valley to tell Elvira that she was making a fool of herself. Now, if there is one thing that Elvira Navarrete is afraid of in this life—I mean, that woman will face snakes and fires, okay?—if there's anything she's afraid of in this life is being thought of, looked on, as a fool. I said: That she was to love Becky's kids as she always has and then I saved the best for last: that she was not going to give Becky any advice at all, today, tomorrow, next year. Elvira was to hush up.

Poor Elvira couldn't keep her eyes off me. Three Pall Mall cigarettes later, and two more jiggers of mezcal to go with them, made the hiccups disappear. Best of all, her voice lost that hysterical squeal she'd brought with her. Not stupid, just high strung.

One has to understand Elvira Navarrete. Some common sense and a little mezcal. But before that? All week long just about everyone was agreeing with her. Not the Ortegóns, of course; others ...

I'm too old not to recognize pride when I see it; Elvira also likes to play the martyr. Hasn't had much reason to, not being married to a womanizer ... All I wanted was to remind her not to listen to everyone, in fact not even to me. To listen to herself, to look at herself. Yes. What was she doing? And for whom? There are too many set phrases in Spanish and English, and they're there ready to come out of some idiotic mouth full of teeth: a poor wife and a worse mother, to begin with. A messy housekeeper; you know the rest. I told Elvira, right here in this porch, she was always welcome, and that she'd bring flowers to my funeral, but until then, she was to cross herself every morning.

And, she was to remember her own mother. That brought her up a bit, I'll say. I then said: "We get enough *caca*-shit-*mierda-cuacha* as it is. And now? You're piling it up and worry about what people will say. What people? Anglos? Hang 'em from a mesquite. Mexicans? Right along with them, I say. Family? What family? Those slave traders, the Leguizamóns? For you, Elvira, there are only five people that matter: Charlie and Sarah, you and Catarino, and Becky. That, Elvirita—and I called her that too—is family."

That's as sharply as I'll ever speak. But Elvira is important in spite of her ridiculous ideas about family and society and such. And then; now? Becky made the right choice, the proper one: she remarried, as I did, as anyone with sense would, if she wanted to marry. She just chose to marry, that's all.

You're related to Jehu, I know that. But where was that boy born? On this land, here, in Relámpago. When his father died, all Jehu had was both parents dead. Try that one on, Elvira, I told her. And that's who Becky chose, decided on.

No, I didn't go back and say Elvira nudged Becky toward Ira, and what for? Now? Elvira wanted comfort, but she didn't know what kind of comfort. Facts are best. No need to change them ... facts and family ... Sometimes the first brings disasters, and the second causes them ... All the time I'm thinking of Macedonio and my father ... Macedonio came here, to this house ... in those days ... that was no easy thing. He had no guarantee how my father would react. *Esos son hombres*. And that Jehu has something of that ... raised differently, but gritty enough.

And that Becky ... came here years ago, with the kids. They're out playing around the house and Becky, looking straight at me says, "I gave myself to Jehu." Married still, of course.

She looked for some sign from me. I didn't say a word. Don't misunderstand, it wasn't that I didn't care, I just wasn't surprised, that's all. I'm too old for surprises, remember? And I won't condone that type of behavior, no matter how old I am. Just that I'm not surprised ... one divorce, a thousand. They're not the end of the world. We've got us a hurricane out in the Gulf right this minute ... so? We had one hit here last year. That one dropped 23 inches of rain. The end of the world? No.

What I told Becky was this: One can't do that, one doesn't go to bed with just anyone. Leave your husband or stay. Don't lie to him. Don't lie to yourself, either. And no confessions, to him or to the Church. Choose, Becky. And she did.

Oh, that Becky ... very Mexican in spite of those Anglo ways of hers ... and her Spanish is a riot. What she says, though, does come from the heart, and I love her for it. And here we sat, on this porch; and I?

I was looking at our family's cemetery wondering who would sit here looking at my headstone ...

I finally shook that off and told her, reminded her, really, that a divorce is just another divorce, that's all that it was. It isn't fatal, it is the reverse: Becky was buying her ransom. She was to be saved, rescued, and with enough love for the kids and for that new husband of hers. A new life for a new woman.

'Cause that's what her Uncle Lionel Villa calls her: *una mujer nueva*. And he, Lionel Villa, he too is a good person; old Valley people those Villas. They've seen the sun rise out of that Mexican Gulf for many years now ...

As for the Anglos, not many understand us, even now. Only way to do so is to marry us, live with us, die with us. But even then, they most likely wouldn't understand us. No, they like to change things around, change the forms of things, and the names of things and places. They're ... they're unstable somehow. *Gente descontenta*, oh, yes.

The listener, a smoker, enjoyed lighting another unfiltered Pall Mall for María de los Reyes Campoy. The listener also drank two thimble-fulls of San Carlos mezcal, "The Best There Is." The listener, from ex-perience, remembers what Un Tal Lucas once said, "There ain't such a thing as good mezcal."

Bill and Tippy Ochoa

Bill and Tippy Ochoa. Friends to Becky before the divorce. He speaks, she nods assent: head, eyes, and mouth all move in union and in approbation. Almost a rehearsal speech it seems. Set phrases. Pauses for emphasis. Brief silence. Etc. The Ochoas are well-known to the listener; Klail City, after all, is Klail City.

I couldn't believe it; let's say I didn't want to believe it. And with all of that education, right. Incredible. Why, I ask you? Why did she do it? To go live with ... with him. Not the same social class, not at all ... I must say that at one time neither Tippy nor I were in Becky's class either, but through hard work and dedication one forms friendships, one is invited here, there ... One can't possibly remain where one starts out. A matter of natural progress, that's all.

Oh, Becky would still be accepted in our circle, no doubt about that, but to marry like that, and to leave Ira? Unwise, wouldn't you say, Tippy? (Eager assent of the head.)

And to think that a Navarrete married to an Escobar blooded to Leguizamón-Leyvas would divorce him and thus lose hundreds of friends? Hundreds of connections? That's quite impossible to understand, am I right, Tippy? (T. nods; Bill Ochoa is then rewarded with a smile.)

I have always said, and I've given it some thought, too, if there is no structure, there can't be any form. In brief, society can't exist, the world as we know it would crumble. Society, respect for institutions, for good manners, the right touch, you understand? That's how people should live. One's people, you understand. Am I not right, Tippy? (A wink from T.)

Let's see. What kind of a married life can Becky and ... and? her new husband expect? I happen to know that he has been known to go into one of those cantinas now and then, those neighborhood cantinas. This is not to say he's a drunkard, by any means ... But, why doesn't he drop in at Chip's or at Cap'n Easy's? A lounge is not a cantina; everyone knows that.

I happen to know that Becky's husband owes a certain loyalty to the Buenrostro family, and that he drinks at those places because his cousin, the policeman, invites him, asks him there. But that doesn't make it right, either. It looks bad.

Mr. Apolinar Tapia, the Notary Public, is absolutely right when he says that to frequent those places is bad form, is to cause a break in the situation of things. The Notary, that's one of his official duties, goes in those places to witness depositions and such. It's part of his job, and it's through him that we learned that Becky's husband goes there. Tippy and I happen to believe firmly that a banker of that rank and status shouldn't be seen in those places. Isn't that true, Love? (Moue and smile from T.)

It must be painful for doña Elvira Navarrete de Caldwell having to hear, having to learn this at second hand. Thank the Lord she doesn't have to witness her new son-in-law going to those places ...

But then, having to know and making comparisons between Ira and him must be a fate worse than Hell itself.

What vice is that? Why the desire and penchant to return to those places? When he was poor, that was understandable. Is it that he is uncomfortable in nice places? No, that can't be it, can it? I mean, not if he's a banker who can go anywhere he likes ... If I was in banking, people would sit up and take notice, I'd make sure of that ... But who am I to complain? Tippy and I own and operate three gift shops, plus the flower shop and some rentals, right, Dear? (The cutest smile followed by the sunniest grin imaginable; a brunette Doris Day, say.)

The listener is not a censor, by any means or stretch. The conversation was brought short by business and by a delivery boy who needed help in the loading and unloading of stock items bearing the "B and T Enterprises" logo.

Gualberto Ornelas, O.M.I.

Gualberto Ornelas, O.M.I. A year before his graduation from Klail High, this future Oblate of Mary Immaculate enrolled in a seminary and began his long study for the priesthood. To date, he is the one young Texas Mexican serving in the Valley. His bishop, Urbano Ortegón, brother to doña Ursula and uncle to Julia Ortegón was the very first Valley Mexican to enter the priesthood; both are Klail City natives.

The listener knows of a third, a native of Jonesville, who is a Jesuit, a serious young man some five years older than Becky's husband, Jehu.

The listener thinks this is a sorry record, given the number of Mexican Catholics in Belken County. The listener, however, sets down facts; some Valley Mexicans find this a disturbing, disgraceful fact.

As the tailoress Otila Macías Rosales says, "This is a truth as big as a whale."

I don't agree with Father Eloy although this should not be taken to mean—nor do I wish to be misunderstood that it mean— that I approve of the divorce. I'm looking for a reconciliation, and if the search, or if the road to it takes time, then, time is what the Mother Church offers all of us as an arm and support against adversity and during times of weakness.

No, I most assuredly do not believe in divorce. I, however, don't hold that divorce is a passport to Hell eternal; I know Father Eloy believes it be so ... and he preaches it; you yourself must have heard him on occasion.

A divorce is harmful to society, and that's where one should start; closer to home. Too, a divorce harms, even torments, the children, if there are any. In Becky's and Ira's case, there are two. There's more to say in this regard, but from what I take it you're interested in, and do stop me if I'm wrong, is that you're a friend to Jehu, as I am. Unlike you, of course, we're not blood relations, but we are friends, and have been since childhood.

That he subsequently married Becky is not only an inconvenience to our friendship, it is also an obstacle. But one must work to overcome inconveniences and obstacles. The Church does not see their living together as constituting a marriage. Living in sin, as Father Eloy would say .... But as for Jehu and me, we're long-time friends. And I'm grateful to him. My late father was a candy maker and he'd lost a leg to diabetes ... My mother had to carry on as best as she could, and Jehu, a teenager as I was, worked for them and for free. *Eso no se olvida* ... And how could I forget that, when I wasn't there, myself, to help? Oh, there's some guilt in me still, but the priesthood is what I had to do, wanted to do ...

Aside from the present bishop, who did not request I come to Klail City by the way, and as far as I know, I may be the only Klail Texas Mexican who's become a priest, an Oblate. That's unfortunate, and I must say this does not reflect well on Holy Mother Church. Don't be offended, but I ask you not to take this as an attack on the Institution. God has His mysteries, and it could very well be that the scarcity of raza in the priesthood to date is a plan to which I'm not privy.

The simple faith I had at seventeen is not the same one twenty-years later; it is, however, as powerful now as it was then.

Jehu and I have truly known each other since infancy, and we were friends, *amigos de amistad*, and we're still friends. I insist on this, because as a priest, I have no enemies, save Satan and unforgiveable sins. Friendship is not a sin nor should one forsake one's friends or neighbors.

I won't be the one to speak of changing the Church, that is to say, to attack it or disagree with it. The day I do, the day I disagree with the determinations and findings of the Church will be the day I hang up the cassock for good ...

But I have faith; I believe in justice, and I also believe that one must work for it, for justice, and one must work in favor of those who are defenseless ... The Church, the Bishop, and I, in my role here, all of us agree in this, although we're not always in agreement as to how to defend people in need.

Father Eloy, and I recognize his kindness, and let there be no doubt about that, his counsels that prayers remain the most ... efficacious remedy in these cases.

For my part, I maintain otherwise, and so I try to have our parishoners help themselves. This is also counseled by the Holy Bible. However, since people are not always prepared to help themselves, I see that as a fault which must be corrected. It's no mystery that they must help themselves, but this doesn't mean that I'm to stay in the rectory waiting for them to come to see me. And so, because of what I feel and believe, I go to their meetings, and that's how I use whatever time I have available.

I did the very same things in Houston and in Laredo, and now, more than twenty years later since I entered the seminary, I now find myself with two years in the Valley, and the last two months of them in Klail.

As for Becky, I hold her in the highest esteem, and for her part, she assists the Church financially. Her actions, to me, are some of the Lord's mysteries, and as long as she lives, she will still be able to change her opinion and return to her husband. This is a fervent hope of mine, and it should be, after all, but I do not keep after Becky on this. She will see and take for herself the proper road, make the correct decision, and she wouldn't be, nor will she be, the first to admit a mistake. It's a transitory lapse.

Her money is both welcomed and accepted, because it's of benefit to all of those who need its benefits. Her children take Mass and to any way of looking at things, this is the first step toward some sort of reconciliation. As for Jehu, and I can't stress enough how long we've been friends, he picks up the boy and the girl as soon as Mass is over. If he doesn't come by, then it's Becky who'll do so. I attach no degree of importance to it, but Jehu doesn't come into the church itself. That's not uncommon in many Valleyites either.

But, when it's monetary matters and we deal with the Klail City First National, Jehu is the one who talks to Father Eloy or with Monsignor Quick. The Monsignor, by the way, isn't unaware of the Escobar family; I mean, the Escobars, particularly in Jonesville, were not only the pillars but also the base of St. Boniface's for years. The bank business is business, it's nothing personal. And really, President Perkins almost always assigns Jehu to these negotiations. They're most delicate, of course, and Jehu posseses marked talents in these regards. And here's something, Jehu himself is a magnet of contradictions. And no, this is neither an attack upon him nor on his methods or his beliefs in any way, and I want that to be understood as well. All it means is that Jehu, nothing more, nothing less, is human.

As for Ira, I'm convinced that he too will return to the Church. He is still on the rolls of this parish, and is one of its assiduous parishoners for over a decade, according to Father Eloy. It's only lately that he hasn't been coming to Mass. It's quite possible, of course, that he is now a parishoner at Jonesville's Sacred Heart, the Leguizamón family parish. Entirely possible.

The listener knows some facts at first hand. The listener also read of and verified the community organizational work of Father Ornelas. Never a pastor with his own church, and always an assistant in the poorest of the poor, this remarkably thin priest, younger in age than his old, tired face betrays, has a talent for being disobliging and for organizing the unorganized. The listener also knows that Father Ornelas has proved an embarrassment to his two past bishops. The first one, in no less a city of consequence than Houston, removed him, exiled is a more proper term, from Houston's notorious Navigation District to a solidly middle class, well-fed, comfortable Mexican American parish in Houston where he languished. The next assignment, Laredo, was a trial for Church authorities: Father Ornelas insisted on working to organize the poor and the needy, unwed mothers, and other so-called social undesirables. The charges against him were that he neglected his religious duties.

His health can't be the best is the listener's opinion. Still, he's a human who does seem to survive by faith alone.

Sammie Jo Perkins

Sammie Jo Perkins, a special item. As tall as the listener, auburn-haired, a ridge of faint freckles dots the nose below some light, light green eyes. Cheek bones? High, as if a Scandinavian's. Thin upper lip, a full-bodied lower one set in an easy smile. Beige silk blouse, long sleeves, no rings on any finger. A gold anchor pendant pinned below a flowing beige silk bow tie.

The listener is fully aware of having given a fairly long description of the persona and the attire. The voice and intonation are Valley products: more U.S. Midwestern than West Texas twang or East Texas drawl.

The Spanish, though, is Northern Mexican-ranch Spanish, smoothed out a bit first at Hollins and later at Smith. An alumna but not a graduate of either; not, as those who know her say, not that she needed to graduate.

The listener has been served a tall, frosted glass of the inevitable Valley limeade. The informant begins.

Spanish was my first language both in the house and of course out in the Ranch. My Daddy, whom I call Noddy more often than not when we get together, speaks Spanish almost as well as I do, but is not at ease in it. For instance, he and I don't speak Spanish to each other as I do, say, with Mamma or with Edith Timmens.

I learned it at home, first from the maids, their kids, the cowboys, Anglos some but mostly Mexican, and later on in Mexico, Spain, and one summer at Smith's summer program in the Baleares ... So, it isn't a matter of talent or a special flair for it; a matter of circumstance. Of the kids I grew up with, Rafe's and my generation, I must be one of

118

the few Texas Anglos who still speaks Spanish. In my mom's generation and Uncle Ibby's too, they spoke it and retained it since it was common practice. But as I said, those of my generation didn't speak it much, but that was their choice, and a poor one at that. Some even bragged about it and now they complain they can't understand a word. Or so they say. In my view, a case of wholesale stupidity. But let's not omit racism since we're dealing known Valley facts, you and I.

And we understand each other, you and I. We both know that Spanish has always been a ticklish affair in the Valley. And so much so that Becky and other mexicanas her age preferred English to Spanish; some were coerced, but this is hard to enforce ... I mean, were the teachers going to follow the kids home? Watch them? Report them? No such thing. Many kids preferred to in many instances, and as a consequence, lost their Spanish, even though their folks spoke little to no English.

In Becky's case, her mother Elvira, seldom uses English, even now. When Captain Caldwell went native, Mexicanized himself, Elvira saw no reason to change. But she made damned sure Becky spoke English, pushed her toward the language. Becky did what most, many, kids did: lost the ability to speak it. Perhaps not the understanding of it ... not when she heard her folks all the time ... Becky preferred English. It's not a crime, but it is a damned shame to lose something which doesn't need to be, but as Rafe says, "You can charge people with stupidity, but they'd be no-billed, there'd be no indictment."

What Elvira did, though, was what numerous Mexican families did, rich and poor alike; they pushed English on the kids. And I see nothing wrong with trying to get on in English, but at the risk and cost of not learning Spanish? That's worse than stupid, that's wrong! Becky herself, and she's a perfect example and product of this, Becky had to make a very special effort to re-learn her Spanish. It wasn't impossible, but she did have to work for it.

I'm on this because I've come to believe that Becky's decision, her changes, let's say, came when she decided to do away with that ridiculous mask. When she did it, she showed us her own sweet face, to put it that way. Using Spanish was part of the restoration ...

And why did she cast Ira off? Who knows? Why does one do anything? I can tell you what I think, but that's not direct knowledge, not at all.

I think she became tired with that cored-shell of a life she was living. And she grew tired of Ira; why not? He is a bore, you know. Duller than battleship gray. Now, that Becky put up with him as long as she did is one of the miracles of the twentieth century. As for Ira, the poor man possesses no sense of humor. There's not a whit of it anywhere in his body. In Spanish or English. Nothing. Nada. Un cero ... A zero. *That's* dull.

What also happened to the younger Becky is that she fell in love with him, Ira, and worse, her mother nudged and pushed them up and down the aisle. That's not what I think; I know ...

Yes, it's irony of the purest kind. Here I am, talking about Becky being pushed into a disaster of a marriage, when I had two disasters of my own. And there is certainly no excuse for either of mine. And I was old too, and one whole hell of a lot more experienced than Becky ... But I was a fool. I allowed Noddy to push me around. And the fault was all mine; I'm supposed to have a mind, a will of my own, and I didn't use either one.

What kept me from winding up at Flora is that through both horrors I didn't forget who I was, wouldn't dream of forgetting who I was. Oh, I swore like a trooper, in public, anywhere. I was a very sick person. Oh, yes. Sick enough to be interned in Flora's asylum.

I got myself into those messes, and it was up to me to get myself out and away from those two damned leeching drones ... What also helps me too is that I'm allergic to alcohol in any form, and since smoking has never been a source of fascination for me, I remained healthy, physically, at any rate.

My life with Rafe, our life, should be no one's concern. Not yours, Noddy's, Mamma's, anybody's. I first saw him when he was fourteen; I'm two years older ... We courted, nothing serious ... but I felt something. Kid stuff, but I also knew it was crazy ... I was crazy. Years later, your cousin Jehu and I had an understanding ... but it wasn't love. We fit; we liked each other.

That Rafe and I didn't marry until twenty years later ranks at the very top of the thousand and one dumb things I've done. I was another Becky too. I didn't have the nerve ... And now I realize I never showed Rafe I loved him. I thought he'd just know.

And now I'm forty and we live together, with a license to prove it ... We're not kids ... living in El Quieto's house, Rafe's house now, and built by his father. That I have a very good part of the money in Belken County comes as no fault of mine, and through no talent, obviously. And no, no more ironies, no coincidences, no soap opera plot by a third-rate writer ... (laughs) make that second-rate. And it's no accident that an heiress—what a word!—of the KBC would marry a Buenrostro. In one of Rafe's books I read where it said that God was funny, that He had a sense of humor ... And you know what? Valley people say the same thing, I've heard it many times ... And so, it's Rafe and I. I'm a born sucker for honorable people. And I married him because he proposed, although I was about to ask him, anyway. It happened there, at the Court House; I'd gone to see him at work, a Friday. I couldn't

have been
there five minutes when he said he was going to see Noddy.

No phony confrontation, just two men, and Rafe with that even, flat voice of his, saying it was time for him to go see Noddy. Well, I told Becky this, same as I'm telling you ... And then it happened two weeks later, certainly no more than that. She salvaged what remains of her life here in Klail. She lanced that carbuncle called Ira Escobar.

And she also left the clubs, those same clubs she would've killed for at one time. I'd left them too ... And what happened to them? Dried up, disappeared. Now there was a lovely piece of sisterhood. And my friends? Which ones? Very few ...

But Becky's decision was a different affair ... and I called her. That's when I began to like her too. And we talked, and talked. Like we'd never done before ... straight, honest talk. Good, earnest talk. But there was a lot of learning, new realizations when the Clubs broke up ...

Look at Heidi Simpson, she divorced Hollis, took little Kimmy or Tiffany, whatever. Returned to school, to earn her own living. And Polly Baxter? Pinkston Baxter never knew what hit him, and Polly took all five kids and left for Lake Charles or some place on the coast. Then there was Nell ... Nell Blankenship. Married for years. Used to not working or having to work ... worse, working like crazy to have a good time. So, there were a few ... and they too changed their lives, as Becky did, as I did ...

The rest? The others? Here, buried alive in Klail City ... where would they go if the Camelot Restaurant closed its doors?

Well ... Becky fooled me too. Fooled herself in the process ... But when she kicked Mr. Commissioner out that door, she removed all doubt. That pretty face was held up by some spine ...

In my case, the easiest thing ... but not in Becky's case. I didn't have to, don't have to answer to anyone ... She did, and she did so, too. You can't help but like someone like that ... And to jump off here, Jehu has always been lucky; and (laughs) I told him so at the wedding ...

Rafe and I waited until Mamma returned from Vail ... her life has been hellish, you know. I think aunt Anna Faye had called her about the Clubs ... Mamma could hardly care if all the clubs in all the world blew up. But Aunt Nellie, Kirpatrick, she, oh, she was not best pleased. And she said some things. Not to my face, of course. But aunt or no aunt, she knows what I'm about ... Meddle in my life? Not a bit of it, but no direct criticism, and not to Noddy either. At least she's learned that.

The one thing Daddy said was that it would be to Aunt Nellie's profit to invest her time and serious efforts in other enterprises than in thinking overlong on her niece. And goodness, when Aunt Nellie learned of Rafe and me ... the end of the world. *El fin del mundo*. But she came to the wedding. See?

And Jehu stood by Rafe, Mamma was my bridesmaid. Wasn't that sweet?

Lunch consisted of a light chicken salad and a phone call from Rafe.

Polín Tapia

Polín Tapia, born Apolinar. He is the Notary Public mentioned by the florist Bill Ochoa. Tapia is a Belken County Court House fixture. Part of the plumbing, as the raza says. Never out of politics, even in off-election years; the listener has been told for years that Noddy Perkins keeps Tapia on some payroll or other. And, as always in those cases, on a short leash. Of course.

Tapia holds himself responsible for Ira Escobar's initial and subsequent elections to the County Commissioner's post (now the gerrymandered Precinct 3), and he also holds himself to blame (though he most certainly shouldn't) for not having Ira in Washington lined up at the federal trough as the Valley's Congressman.

The listener finds Polín entertaining, interesting, even. Biased people usually are an interesting species. And, as most egotists, entertaining, although not for long.

Let me begin by stating in the strongest terms possible that Becky Escobar committed a grave error in divorcing Ira. Her inability to see the man's qualities, in my way of thinking, denotes a lack of foresight, a lack of judgment, and a marked inability in the most important realm there is, the ability to read people. To think that after some eleven years of marriage she didn't acquire, couldn't focus on the type of person Ira was and is, is to set her off apart. Yes, that says it all for Becky Escobar, or rather, Malacara now ... This last really tears it for me; beyond belief, is how I put it.

Yes. Incredible, inconceivable that that girl who appeared to have everything going for her, that she lost her head, stumbled, and then only to fall into Jehu's arms and hands.

No. It's witchery of some kind. A thing of magic dust and powder to blind that poor girl somehow.

Yes. It's easy for one to believe that, easier still to accept such a supposition. I'm not saying Jehu is a warlock or something like that, but there's something there. I don't know what though. An intrigue of some sort. Something sinister; got to be.

It must be that, otherwise, how can you or I or anyone explain why she left Ira? Hmph ... Ira Escobar is a model, a prototype. No, no, no, no! Becky lost her head; a moment of transitory madness, no two ways about it. I can't find any other reasonable explanation.

And for what, I ask you? So she could then go live with Jehu Malacara? I mean, really now ... I certainly thought her to be a sensible girl ... I thought of her as someone serious, yes. Jehu Malacara! Well, as for me, I rise at six every morning, and as soon as my feet hit the floor, I ask myself how is it that God hasn't found out about that guy. Because that's what Jehu Malacara is, a guy.

And then, to see, year after year, how Noddy Perkins puts up with him at the Bank ....Oh, no, there's got to be something there. Got to be some big, fat, thick mystery. Worse than that for all I know. What I fail to see is that so-called talent of his. Where is it? I'm open-minded, and if someone can prove it to me that Jehu has a spark of talent, then I'll be a convert too. But I've yet to see it, no matter how many people say he has it.

What talent, Dearest Lord? Which one? Where? How? No, no. It's a myth, a mystery. Talent? I'd gladly hand over all the riches of the Orient if I could ever see his so-called talent.

Talent? I'll give you talent: Ira, he's the one. Upstanding young man, good family background, educated, proper, efficient. Someone who has served this County precinct in his political duties and obligations.

I taught him what I know about politics, but I soon saw that he wasn't merely a good learner; Ira Escobar could be a teacher of it in some college. And I tell him so, repeatedly: "Ira, you are one of the chosen. To be a commissioner in the County Commissioner's Court, in Belken County, is not just anything. No sir."

If one, quite objectively now, compares Belken with Dellis County, we'll use Dellis as an example, then there's no comparison. And there he is, Ira Escobar, governing the important business of the County. Belken, as St. Paul would say, is no mean city. We are talking here of one of the most important counties in the whole of South Texas. Yes, without a doubt.

All right. Fine. What can you tell me about Becky? Hmph. There she is. Sweeping the Escobar name as if through a dirt floor in the poorest farm. And worse, oh yes. Dragging and hauling the kids wherever she goes ... Really, now. She takes them here, she takes them there. I ask you, seriously: What kind of a mother is that?

Can Jehu Malacara pass out advice? No, no, no. I'm telling you: the world is breaking up, coming unraveled. There's no structure anymore. That's right. The divorce is but one hint among many of what's happening in the world today ...

What more can one say, right? Now, one would suppose that Sammie Jo could well help Becky, to guide her, let's say. And maybe she did, and maybe she was turned away, right? And seeing how the world is nowadays, and Becky's perverse state of mind, why, anything is possible.

In a pragmatic way, let us say, I don't believe the divorce has hurt Ira. The elections are looming in the very near future, almost like that hurricane out in the Gulf right now. Looming. Threatening ... Where was I? Ira, yes. Well, Ira remains faithful to his political ideals, and I've just devised—paraphrased—a new slogan for him, and you should hear Ira, in that natural, loose, but controlled way of his when he speaks to his Spanish-speaking constituency: "Effective voting, down with corruption!"

How's that, eh? From my own pen and ink, and with echoes of the heroes of the Mexican Revolution.

But life is long, not short, and carries with it its consequences. True enough, and you hold on to that. That girl will meet a sad, unhappy ending, although I certainly wish her nothing mean or evil, and I want that to be shouted from the top of Our Lady of Mercy or even downtown, from the third floor of the Klail First National. I wish Becky only the best ...

But a bad ending is inevitable, and it's sad because I admire some of her qualities. But I'm a realist, and one has to be a realist. All you have to do is see what company she keeps: Viola and Jehu. And then what does she do? She resigns from her duties in important women's clubs. Klail Society. That can't possibly lead to any good for anyone. Just wait and see.

And, I should very much wish to point out that Ira won't lose any ground because of those resignations two years ago. The divorce wasn't his idea; everyone knows that, takes it into account. So, as a result, Ira came out unharmed, let's say ... it was Becky's disaster, not his.

In personal matters, that is an entirely different subject ... let it also be said that I am Courtesy Itself in all my dealings with Becky. I harbor no rancor. You like the phrase? My behavior is that which the Tapias have always maintained: rectitude, honesty, and loyalty to all institu-

tions. As for Becky, I give her all of my counsel and advice. To date,
I've no evidence she has ever followed anything I've ever said. But one
does what one can. Yessir. One fulfills one's duties and obligations. Do
we understand ourselves here?

That she chooses to follow her own counsel and advice, as poor or
harmful as they may subsequently prove to be, that, unfortunate as it
may be, is not an immediate concern of mine. But if it were, if … it
were, I would be the first to offer my services and my advice as to how
she should proceed.

But no, this won't come to pass. It's impossible for me to help her
as long as she lives with Jehu. And married, some say.

Well, say what they may, say whatever it is they wish to say, how can
anyone believe such a union is marriage?

She'll learn, poor Becky. She'll learn of his eccentricities, his incon-
stancy. Yes, she'll see Jehu Malacara for what he is.

In a word, there is no comparison between Ira and Jehu. None. No
sir.

What Becky does have, unquestionably, unhesitatingly, and close at
hand, at any time, is the unconditional, disinterested friendship of one
Apolinar Tapia.

Yessir.

The eye of the storm, no, no, Apolinar Tapia is not the eye of the
storm … , rather, the real eye of the storm, in the words of Julia Ortegón's brother, the weatherman, is "calm, but the area outside the eye
is packing winds of 125 miles an hour." The weatherman also reports
that tornadoes are to be expected when the hurricane hits land. This
last, however, is not known where or when it will occur.

Noddy Perkins

The listener has an appointment with Noddy Perkins. Powerful personality, restless, edgy, inclined to make nervous those around him. Pure upmanship.

Proud and loving father to Sammie Jo, and husband to Blanche Cooke.

The red face and its red scalp with a shock of white hair remain in place.

The listener may, perhaps not, but the listener may have omitted to point out the strong chin and a slight, but deep scar above the right side of his upper lip. The listener has not found anyone who knows how the scar came about. It's an old scar, the only piece of non-red tissue in his face.

Fine restorative dental work there, by the upper lip. Eyes, a soft, royal blue. They appear incongruous, given that strong nose and the stronger chin, but the penetrating look of the eyes attests power; the listener has formed the opinion that Perkins has decided, perhaps trained himself, to blink as little as possible.

The listener intrudes and explains here because the elections are "looming" (Cf. Tapia) and the listener wishes to hear, learn, at first hand what Noddy Perkins has to say about the Commissioner.

Ira Escobar is a fine young man. He does good work as a County Commissioner, and I've no objection at all regarding his private life, either.

I know there are people who say we run him like a sheep dog, but I don't see it that way.

I'm a businessman, and I want the Valley to prosper. If a Mexican can be helped on his way to occupy a local political post, the county is a good example; that's what we're here for.

Ira's transfer to our branch in Jonesville was most convenient. We're in the same precinct after the last reapportionment and his residency in Jonesville suits him. He's in no danger of losing his seat. The *Enterprise-News* certainly holds that view.

Ira is a serious young man and carries out his duties. To add to this, he has some sensible ideas which help him see his duties clearly.

My policy is not to meddle in my employees' private lives; I've nothing more to say on this. I'm not cutting you off here exactly, it's that my chief concern is running the Bank. I've three or four appointments this afternoon also . . .

Now, if you have some time, let's go across to El Fénix for some coffee. I'll flip you for it.

The listener prefers the Perkins Treatment than to being hustled by easy language. Note: the listener won the coin toss for coffee but lost the pastry toss. To quote Jehu Malacara: When going against Noddy, in anything, a tie tastes as good as a win.

Nora Salamanca

Next, the formidable Nora Salamanca. Eyes? Blue black. Hair, graying and with a bluish tint. Height: 5' 4" and weighing in at 125 lbs. By Valley Mexican and Anglo standards, not an old family, but old enough. Gaspar Nieto and María de la Concepción Hirsch (de Nieto) say that the first Salamancas came to the Valley around the time of the War of '98. The Salamancas, to a man and woman, came to the Valley as members of the merchant class; this is still the case. N.S. is married to Pascual Navarrete.

It seems quite impossible for such a well-educated girl as my niece, Becky Escobar, certainly is, to have thrown away her life just like that; out the window, as we say. Too, I'm convinced that she was in the wrong, and that someone handed her some bad advice; otherwise, how can anyone explain to me that rash, abrupt decision of hers?

Notary Public Polín Tapia, by the way, calls on us once in a while. Always respectful towards all members of this household, Polín speaks and says many truths. As I say, if that man had been afforded a formal university education, no telling where he'd be by now.

At any rate, getting back to Becky. I see a sinister hand here. That decision could not have come out of Becky's mouth alone, unless, of course, a something or a someone or some nefarious spirit entered her mind and soul . . .

What she did, to rid herself of as good a man as Ira Escobar, is not the decision made by a woman who's in control of her senses, a woman so created by the Lord.

I have no earthly idea what got into that girl's head. I'm not saying that she should have been a slave, no, not at all; however, her actions may lead, influence, other girls to consider the same thing with their lives. And what if we do come to that pretty pass? What then? I ask you.

Why bother having *familias directoras*, being the leading families? I ask you. How are we to serve as an example to others? What will the Anglos think? I ask you. And, who will we have to lead in the future?

Women can vote, can't they? And they can own property, right? Well? What else do they want? Becky is and was raised spoiled, whatever she wanted was always handed her. And now? Well, now she has to earn a living, but at what cost to her position? And, she's going to have to learn what it means to work. To have to compete. What it means to bring food to the table. And, do you honestly think a woman, so raised, can actually earn a living? I ask you.

I truly hope she can avoid the suffering, but what she did isn't right at all. And how can it be right when by her own selfish actions, she just did away with one of the most important social laws: to remain at the side of a man who could provide for her, who could stand guard over her, as society has been observing for saecula saeculorum?

It's a bad piece of business is what it is. An enterprise which will end badly, and I say this sadly, even if, at the same time, I recognize I'm right.

First of all: the children need their father. And just what is it that those two poor innocents have to see, day after day? What a perfectly, lovely example, isn't it? Seeing their mother living with your relative, cousin is it? Well, relative anyway ... with that not-quite-right-in-the-head Jehu Malacara. From all I hear, about your cousin, it's an ever-lasting miracle he's not been run off from the Bank for a second time. That's right, a miracle.

Jehu Malacara, and you must excuse my bluntness and my frankness, I'm just built that way, is not the proper person to raise children, and less still, to raise someone else's children.

Now you see why I'm convinced that there's something sinister about all this? Witchcraft, even? And don't you doubt that for a minute, either. There's something hiding near the woodpile ... And I'll tell you this, too: time will tell, it always does.

I've known Ira for years and years, and his family before that, and let me stress and underline that there's excellent blood in that lineage, a good, healthy breed. The Leguizamóns— and Ira is one on his maternal grandmother's side—are steadfastly honest and honorable. Exactly.

I know, I know there are some who would and do try to discredit their good names. Those are the words of pernicious rumormongers. The Leguizamóns have always behaved as the gentlemen they are. Gen-

erous, unstinting in the charitable projects, freehanded in their contributions to Holy Mother Church ... a sense of honor that thrills all
believers to witness such probity, such openhandedness in giving away
their earthly goods. There's a long line of people who'd love to measure
up to those standards, oh yes.

And if one must swear on the Bible, I swear I saw that Caldwell-
Navarrete union with the Escobar-Leguizamón-Leyva as something designed by heaven. I swear it. Anyone who could have foreseen that
marriage would have forecast nothing but the very best for that young
couple. Exactly.

But now? And with that war in China, wherever ... And the few
Mexicans in college acting up? What's this country coming to? What's
this world coming to? And now Becky divorcing ... the end of all the
good things on earth is close at hand. We, thank the Lord, have no
relatives fighting in that country. But what kind of an example are the
present mexicanos presenting to the Anglos? Long hair, longer than
some of the girls. And the girls, the way they dress in college? Whatever
happened to modesty, to clean hands and clothes, I ask you? They're
supposed to be in school to learn!

And now, Becky in a divorced state. Now, if what I'm about to say
isn't too out of place, I would repeat what I said earlier, since, surely,
others are saying it now. Becky's actions are not those of someone who
is mentally balanced.

I do not mean to say that she's deranged, or that she's one of those
who doesn't care about what people say. Not at all. What I do mean,
however, is that I am not entirely convinced that Becky wasn't drugged
or influenced by something, a someone, by that nefarious force I spoke
of. In times such as these and that war and all, no one who understands
these things could possibly disagree with me.

I would be the last person to claim to know the exact reason, but is
it possible that Jehu Malacara drilled a hole in her head and sucked out
every bit of sense she ever had? Your cousin isn't a monster, nor do I
suggest that, but it's all beyond me.

Oh, I know that talking this way sounds just as crazy or as someone
who is still living in the past century ...

As for Jehu ... I'm just saying and say what our friend Polín Tapia
says. He knows him far better than I do, of course, and all I do is quote;
you mustn't hold it against me. He asks what other people ask: who is
Jehu Malacara? Better still, he says, what is Jehu Malacara? And the
answer is nothing, a Mr. Nothing. I won't go that far, but that's what
Polín Tapia says.

But he asks just what many of us ask. And then, to have him at
the Bank! At the KBC Ranch's own Klail First! What possible talents

could he have been born with? And if he does possess some talents, where does he keep them, hide them?

On the other hand, Ira Escobar is a talent. That my niece Becky is blind to it is a different matter altogether. Ira not only worked at the Bank, he's now at the Savings and Loan, and then, when you add that fine public service, you'll see exactly what I mean. There's a wide gap between the two men.

And frankly, it's the children I feel for. Thank goodness that Dalia is here. It's not because she's my sister's daughter, but at times I wish Ira would've had more luck in his choice of partners in his twenties ... Dalia Ramos-Botín would have been my choice, and still is. There's her picture: as nice and as beautiful as ever, and she's two years younger than Becky, too.

I won't be the one to get those two together, but in all truth, aside from being my niece, as is Becky, I don't see anyone else who belongs to the same social category. Do you?

Poor Ira. That boy never knew what hit him. Elvira Navarrete herself paved the road, laid the tracks, and engineered the entire affair. I've never seen the equal to that sister-in-law of mine. She moved half the world to get her way so that Becky would marry Ira.

I'm not criticizing Elvira; she did what she had to do and what she thought was right as a mother. And I'll be the first to say so. What is a bother, though, is that Elvira herself was blinded, yes, even she didn't see all of Ira's merits, all his good points.

This is not to say that Becky is entirely without her own plusses, or that Ira was better or even too good for Becky. Not at all. What Becky failed to see back then, though, was that Ira's brilliant future lay before them, calling to them. She'd set her sights too low, from the beginning. In a word, she didn't strive hard enough toward Ira's success.

Oh, she had those two darling kids, she joined some clubs and all, and that's beyond reproach, obviously. But anyone could see that what she wanted was independence. A bit selfish, she just didn't do more for Ira.

And how did she wind up? Well, see for yourself. Working for that señora, that, that, that Viola Barragán. As I've always heard repeatedly, one cannot be too careful in choosing one's friends ... Anybody who is anybody knows and admits that Elvira and the Barragán woman became great friends years and years ago. As to how Elvira has remained close to her, even now, is the mystery of mysteries. And poor Becky? With that woman as a model for her? But it just so happens that Becky doesn't have to work. And if she has to work, and she's working now and has been almost since that tragic day, why must it be with that woman? Of all people. I ask you.

Yes, oh, yes. And talking of a poor choice of friends, Jehu, your cousin, as so well you know, travels in that same Barragán orbit. No doubt on that at all. Everybody knows how that woman has taken him under her wing, for years now. And maybe that's what accounts for Becky's downfall: The Barragán woman pushed and shoved and schemed to get your cousin and Becky together. I ask you.

Let all of us pray that Becky's affair doesn't give rise to some unfortunate incident, that something bad awaits her. Although you must admit that a large part of Becky's fault in all of this is due to her insistence to work. Well? Doesn't she have enough work at home? No one required her to resign from the clubs.

A family grows, is nurtured in the hearth with the man defending the family home and its honor, and the woman, as always, reigning as his faithful partner. Exactly. My Pascual and I must be an example of what I'm talking about.

When my sister Norma died, I raised Dalia, and favorite niece or not, she knows what keeping and maintaining a house is all about. She's also respectful, highly modest, and very good looking, too.

Ira Escobar would have to travel to China and back before he could hope to find someone as suitable as Dalia. As regular as the sun, she is a devout believer, and that too is essential and thus a requirement for a Christian household. Hardworking, industrious, she's also respectful, highly modest, and very good looking, too. My niece is not, as we say in Spanish, *una pelagatos*, someone who skins cats for a living. She's graceful, she carries herself well, and you're hearing from one who knows. Blood kin or not, my assessment doesn't enter into this. She has her own very good points, as I never tire of telling any one.

But as far as Becky is concerned, nothing good comes for those who behave as she did. Yes, straying off morality's well-paved high road is bound to bring something ill, something dangerous ... But as I said, God forbid ...

What's galling, though, is to have to see Becky lowering herself. You know, I think we women are our worst enemies sometimes ... and tell me this, is Becky working for what some people call progress? God help us!

The listener lost some notion of time and thought. It was time for a final cigarette and a drink. The listener, tired and all, found that food, not drink, was called for. Food was not offered at the Salamanca home;

the listener ate shortly after and felt rejuvenated, if not in a spiritual sense.

Matías Soto, O.M.I.

Matías Soto, O.M.I. Native of Boiro, in Spanish Galicia. Living, praying and saving some selected souls in the Valley for over twenty years. A high-pitched, almost hysterical, raspy voice accompanies a perennial five'o clock shadow on a very white, very pale face.

No, I agree, one divorce more or less does not mean or signal the end of the world, nor will the world lose its place in the galaxy, but you must admit that a divorce may very well destroy the welfare of any family which has enjoyed the Church's blessing.

The unsettling part in this serious affair, however, is that Becky didn't ask or seek for a way to have prevented what she did. At the first sign of trouble, she could have come here for solace and counsel. That's what we're here for, after all. She committed an error of judgment, a fault, let us say. She acted poorly.

Didn't she trust me? The Church? As a mother, Becky's first thoughts should have been as they should always be, for the family's welfare. Ira isn't blameless, either, you know, but women are the first bastion, the principal base and foundation of the Church family. That is not a debatable point. But, Ira, as a man and father, had his obligations, goodness knows. Oh, I can well understand his error and his willful pride, another error, of trying to resolve everything alone and without advice from any quarter. But it so happens I know both of them, and in spite of the fact that they changed to the Anglo parish when they moved from here to Klail, I was always, as I am now, ready to listen and to help them resolve their problems.

The Sisters now tell me that the children are no longer enrolled in

135

their school, and that is an error. Why are they to bear any blame for any of this? But I guess that's what always happens in these cases, one precipitous ill-conceived action that . . .

As for Becky, I fail to see the reason why she disenrolled the children. And even less now, when they are in more need than ever of spiritual guidance. Yes, now, when the children need the help and support of our institutions, the Church's institutions.

But all of this was done on the spur of the moment, surely; it came upon as sure as that hurricane out in the Gulf will land here tonight, or tomorrow. Happy as larks one moment and then unhappy in the twinkling of a bird's eye. It's the times, these times! The Church sees herself threatened on all sides. And don't you remember, not too long ago, that assassination attempt in the Philippines on His Holiness Pope Paul? And then that horrible war in French Ind— in Viet Nam? A Catholic country soon to be in the deadly grip of Communists and Communism? The Church has every right to feel threatened, beset. Lord, Lord, it's the times.

To give you an idea, I am the last Spanish Peninsular priest in the Valley . . .

That's right; the Irish are returning to the Valley, and now the Texas Mexican faithful will be left to shift for themselves all over again. But as I've said, it's these times . . . Listen to this, how many new churches have been erected in Klail or Bascom, let's say, or in Jonesville, the largest city in the Valley? The number is zero plus zero.

And now? What? Well, two very important mexicanos divorced! What an example on their part! Bad business, bad, bad . . .

But what is to be done? As for me, I'm no longer either surprised or shocked by anything. Just as soon as we dispensed with Latin, that signaled the inevitable crumbling of forms, believe me. This is an institution, and more than that, a holy institution with special rites, forms, and its special history.

Oh, yes. Holy days, fasting before communion, the confession as a private sacrament, and more . . . all of this heaved as so much trash on some country road. Well, we still have our doctrine, but if catechism classes are suspended, we may as well close the doors and turn our churches into museums, I say.

That's right, and while young and socially influential couples like the Escobars do not take the reins of moral leadership, what can we expect from the rest of the parishioners? Oh, yes, I know that the majority of our parishioners make up the very foundations of the Church, but they still need the models such as those provided by the sons and daughters of the *clases directoras*.

And now? To begin with, one less acolyte, since Charlie is no longer a member of this parish, and worse, Father Thomas now tells me that Charlie is not serving at masses in his parish in Klail.

That may just be another signal that Baby Sarah will no longer be helping the Dames of the Perpetual Candle Society ... I must say that Becky probably didn't even stop to consider as to what would take place on account of her precipitous action.

This parish certainly will not close its doors to her when and if she repents with all her heart and after she's undergone an examination of conscience with cleansed, sane thoughts proving, too, that everything is in place. We're not living in the era of the Inquisition, goodness knows; we're flexible and ever ready to embrace the fallen. We live and work with human beings who are, after all, imperfect because of their humanity. It's because of this knowledge in mind that we are always disposed to help those who've suffered some transient, momentary lapse. It all has to do, let there be no doubt, with saving souls and with praying that they attain a personal conviction of the Holy Faith. And too, how is one to know that this is just one test on the part of the Lord? Anything is possible. There exist many mysteries in this world, and let's all pray that Becky take measure of herself and her actions, and that she direct her feet on the road to righteousness. And do please forgive my having to leave at this moment, but I've some parish affairs I must attend to.

The listener thanked Father Soto for his time. The listener plans to wait two days before driving to Jonesville. Mrs. Elvira Navarrete de Caldwell has kindly consented to talk to the listener.

Elvira Navarrete

Elvira Navarrete (de Caldwell). Becky's mother.

Thanks be to God and to all His Angels, and the consolation they bring, but I see Becky's divorce as the Lord's punishment. God Himself knows why He's inflicting this pain on me, and that's why I've resigned myself to see this as further proof of my faith. And, I can't possibly be in better hands in this travail! Father Soto has brought consistent consolation and advice during this tragic occasion. Although it's been over two years since the divorce, I manage to live my life from day to day ...

As you so well know, Becky has gone off and married that, that Jehu person, and then? In a civil ceremony! Yes, yes, and yes, I know perfectly well who he is, and I most assuredly do not need Viola's reassurances and details as to his background.

And Viola is my oldest and my very best friend, and now she talks to me of "your son-in-law, Elvira," and she wants me to convince myself to accept him. It's been difficult, don't you see? Viola and I are friends, but despite that, I'm not going to fully accept that man or even follow, let alone take, Viola's advice. But whatever else you may have heard to the contrary, I do talk to him.

Father Soto let me know that my acceptance of this second husband could well occasion the most gravest consequences. That's what he said. I, I, I didn't even stop to ask him what they could be ... but the Church is all powerful and she knows the answer. And what am I supposed to do? He brings Charlie and Sarah here ... they can't very well walk here from Klail, can they?

And Catarino? You could well have asked me, yes. That husband of mine is blind, since birth, I would say, blind to any fault of Becky's. His baby is always right! Can you imagine? Why, if it hadn't been for me, Becky and Ira would have never married, believe me. To wait, to have to depend on Catarino to make a move in that direction, would have been to wait for a snowfall in the Valley ... To wait for a miracle, to put it that way.

Catarino knows a lot about a lot of things, but he doesn't have the slightest notion of how to go about engagements, marriages ... Not the slightest. He is a good man, as decent as you'll ever find, but it's almost impossible to introduce anything like this into that head of his.

Of course, since he was raised as a Protestant, what does he understand of a Catholic conscience? Oh, he reads that Bible there, but what's that to me? That has absolutely nothing to do with me, I'm no Bible-thumper; I'm a Catholic woman and very Catholic, and yet, for two years now, I stand here, watching the world go to pieces all around me. But my faith and Father Soto's advice see me through during these difficult events ...

And Becky? My, my darling little girl, my baby, has fallen in error, and she won't let me cry to my heart's content and relief.

"None of that, Mama," she says. "You can cry in front of your friends, and all you want, too."

Can you believe that from her?

And now trying to talk in Spanish, yes. She, who speaks English just like the Anglos; identically. And she still speaks it, of course, but she says that Spanish is important to her. Is that true? Where did she get that idea?

Well now, I'm a mexicana, and my husband an americano, and our household is also mexicano. Becky attended the Catholic school, and the Sisters taught her English just like the Anglos, but you must know we never stopped using Spanish. But as far as I'm concerned, and Father Soto, too, it's that love of money which is at the root of all this ... this corruption. Well, not corruption, really, but at the heart of the end of that marriage. Oh, what God has united, what God has united ...

You see, Ira calls on me, faithfully. He behaves as what he is, a gentleman. As for Becky, she'll lose those blinders, she'll see the light.

And I can tell you, as I'd tell the world, too, that that second marriage is not a legal act. It could very well be annulled, as Father Soto assures me. The Church would do it for us, for the family ... Father Soto says the proceedings would probably take some time, and perhaps some financial resources by way of a gift to the parish, but I tell you, whatever would be given would be as nothing for their eventual reconciliation.

And what does Becky say to this? "What a hope!" Dear God, at times she says some things that'll rattle your teeth. But all of this is perfectly understandable in an unstable state, as Father Soto says. At times, too, Becky says that Jehu, Jehu Malacara, that Jehu is a man, and you should hear how she says it, "A man!" As if that were something special, right? Well, isn't Ira a man, too? And isn't her own father a man? There's no way to understand young people today.

And the children? What can I possibly tell you? Happy as they can be with their Mom, oh, yes. And, since this house is the one place Ira can call on them, that's where you'll see them . . .

Charlie? You'll find his nose stuck in a book somewhere, and you can't get a word out of him. Baby Sarah? She listens to what her Dad says with as much attention as I pay to the wind outside. Oh, she sits close to him, but she could well be in the next county. She'll wander into the kitchen, helps me make some chocolate, sets the table and all, and she does it smiling and humming, but I don't think her heart is in kitchen work at all. But when it comes to respect, she, and Charlie, too, they are respectful as can be to their father. But when Ira leaves, why, it's like he's never been here at all.

I think that's strange. And me? Well, I'm Grandma, Mamá Grande, and Catarino is Grandpa . . . I know they love their father and all, but you should see them when they talk about Jehu. And how can I even think of stopping them from talking of Jehu in this house? That isn't done, and I will not be the one to put a stop to that. One has one's religion, true, but there's social courtesy too, you know.

Don't think of me as a crazy person, but I fail to see or understand what it is that Becky sees in Jehu Malacara. You can't say he's good-looking. That rather smallish nose has a decidedly Jewish hook to it. Eyes? A light green, I think. A sort of erased look about them, gray, perhaps. As for the rest, regular features, nothing outstanding, to speak of. A bit taller than Ira, thin-like, while Ira has the Leguizamón look with that cute little stomach bulge which suits him quite well. Gives him an air of respectability, don't you think? Jehu is nondescript. Period.

And Becky says Jehu is a first-rate banker, although, in the very few times I've spoken to him , I don't find him smart at all . . . I don't know . . . I have a very good idea what a banker should look like, be like . . . like Ira, for instance. And as far as I'm concerned, Jehu Malacara doesn't even look like a banker. He's just like Noddy Perkins.

That Noddy Perkins looks like something plucked from a cotton field not fifteen minutes ago: red-faced, red-necked . . . He looks like a field hand to me, and yet Becky says that according to Jehu, Noddy Perkins knows banking from the ground up. Well, you could've fooled me . . . Oh, and Noddy speaks Spanish, yes he does. I've not one clue as to his family background, where he came from, but since he married someone from the Ranch, he must have some lineage to him. In those affairs, the Ranch crowd is mighty cautious, you know.

It may sound strange to you, but Becky doesn't care one whit about any of that. She says that for her, people are people, and that's it. For example, her friendship with Sammie Jo Perkins is as strong as ever, stronger perhaps. That americanita is a bit, no, not a bit, she's very, actually, too independent for my likes. She scares me at times ... But she and Becky get along just fine, thank you. And even more and better now. Becky also assures me they get along so well because of a solid friendship, and because of, of that, ah, that new life of Becky's.

A life, let me tell you, that I do not understand. But I will say this too, if the kids are happy, and I certainly see them that way, and as long as Becky isn't hurt, I'm her mother after all, I'll be happy and at peace, and I'll just wait until she sees the light. I'll have you know Becky won't allow me to talk this way, about seeing the light. And she says, the little devil, that she *has* seen the light. Can you imagine? That she saw the light, and that she likes it, and I don't just know what all she does say. But, in spite of everything, and I do mean everything, Becky is not a bad person, thanks be to God.

The phone rings, and the listener makes for another room, only to be stopped by a wave of the hand. Doña Elvira Navarrete points to the television set and signals it be turned on; cupping the mouthpiece, doña Elvira wants to listen to a weather report. The phone call, from a neighbor, perhaps, is a short one, and both the listener and Becky's mother listen to the most recent stalling of the hurricane some eighty-five miles southwest of Jonesville.

After this, strong coffee and some homemade *empanadas de cala-baza*.

Raúl Santoscoy

Raúl Santoscoy. A cousin of Jehu; also Jehu's fellow university student; currently a pharmacist and rancher/farmer.

i

Jehu? For years? Since we were kids. As for Becky, only since she and Ira first came to Klail, and what facts I picked up at the time, and that was common knowledge. That's all changed, of course.

In all truth, I didn't care for her when they first blew in here from Jonesville. I met him first, and I sure didn't like him from the get-go. And then, I went ahead and just thought she'd be cut from the same cloth. And I held on to that until I had a long talk with Viola Barragán. That's been years, though, and by then Jehu'd left the Bank and the Escobars were cutting that wide, loud swath of theirs. It was about then, I think, that Viola'd come over to see me and my dad about leasing some land for a couple of seasons. As you know, I don't farm much on this side of the River; my cousin Rafe and I farm some together, but mostly, we farm on the Mexican side. Our families been doing that for years, so what's new? ... and now you got Anglos farming on the other side, too. I guess they'll always be with us, like St. John says ...

Well, as it usually turns out on those visits from town, we had some supper, a few drinks, and as always, too, a lot of politics. The usual. Well, Viola isn't much of a drinker to speak of, and though the talk happened a long time ago, and I can't remember what my uncle Blas said, but I'm sure it had to do with County politics, all of a sudden Viola cut in. She said something like this: " ... it seems to me that Elvira Navarrete's little girl is the one with the brains in that marriage."

She said it again after supper, and what impressed me was that Viola felt very sure of what she was saying. And that from a woman who doesn't like to hear herself talk.

I sure hadn't thought or remembered that dinner years ago until the Escobars separated. But that was then, and now, Becky's married to my cousin Jehu. I was a *padrino*; I stood for him, and I made most of the arrangements too. I called Judge Treviño, the restaurant, and so on. I also got to see Becky a heck of a lot and certainly more than I had in the past eight to nine or however many years it was.

So I changed my mind about her; I liked what I saw: a serious woman and her two kids at the right side next to Jehu. She kissed him and then the kids right after the ceremony. She shook my hand, firmly too, then she hugged Viola and Mr. and Mrs. Caldwell. We'd all crowded into Ramón Treviño's chambers, and then she hugged old Hinojosa, the attorney. From there, straight to the restaurant for a smallish reception.

My wife was already there, and she'd brought her sister, Julia, and aunt Ursula. Casa Cordoba, of course. And first thing, Jehu opened some double doors and Charlie and Sarah went off somewhere, like the three had planned it ahead somehow. At any rate, the rest of us sat down for breakfast and everything.

As Rafe says, and this is worth noting: Judge Treviño didn't make a fool of himself. I remember Jehu laughing and saying that there hadn't been enough time for that. Anyway, after the last toast, Jehu and Becky and the kids drove out to the beach.

Oh, one thing. Right before they all left, Jehu handed me a sealed envelope. No idea how he got 'em, but inside there were four tickets for the season's top bullfight. Eloy Cavazos, no less. There were some lottery tickets too, and Jehu'd hit the last numbers twice, so I got some forty bucks back! Ese Jehu ...

Well, my dad died some six months after the wedding, and I sold my dad's part of the pharmacy to my cousin, Beto Chayres. And then before the year was out, Beto's kids moved to Houston, away from the Valley, Beto himself retired, and then turned around and sold the drug store to Viola. Well, I happen to know for a fact that Becky also runs that end of the business, because Viola again drove out to see me and to ask whether or not that was a solid enough investment.

I said it was and added that I'd sell her my twenty percent ... it all fit like a handmade glove. Old Hinojosa is Viola's favorite lawyer, and since he represented Becky in the divorce ... Old Romeo told me to keep the deed to the building to which Viola agreed, then I just rented it out to her and it worked out well for all.

Now, Jehu's no lawyer, but he had a big hand in that transaction. He then asked me to work at the pharmacy on salary, say twenty hours a week, part time, and Viola saw that I made out all right. A fine arrangement, and the Bank, you can't escape that, made some money, but that's part of Jehu's job, too.

And now Martín San Esteban is talking about wholesale pharmaceuticals. Told him to go ahead, I'm no competition to him. With what Rafe and I farm and now me working for myself and for Viola under the arragement, those twenty hours in town are enough. I can do them any which way I want to: a weekend, two days in a row, three ... it doesn't matter. After farming, it's nice to get inside a place. Sure is.

The listener and Raúl Santoscoy went across the street for afternoon coffee and rolls. That took half an hour.

ii

As for Jehu, it's about time he had some luck ... There he was, thirty-something, and he finally meets and falls in love with Olivia San Esteban, and then to have her die that stupid death ... Man! But good luck had to come his way, sometime. Becky saw in him what Viola and Noddy both had seen right from the start, a man without a price. Hmph. Damned Noddy finally gave up trying to get my cousin into County politics ...

And that's a major difference. Ira lapped it up. Talk about limitations.. Talk about not knowing one's own limitations. He doesn't quite have the reach, you know. He's got some things going for him, but my wife says he lacks something. I married one of those Ortegón women and there's not much they don't know ...

Now that we're on Ira, maybe there isn't a word to describe or to sort him out with. Maybe that's why Carmen says to let it go. And of course there isn't a drop of Anglo blood in him, and yet he's not a mexicano. Explain that.

Let me tell you a story: during his first election, I didn't let the political workers staple Ira's flyers on our fence posts. That's not much, just a couple of miles on the Military Highway give or take. Now, you and I know Noddy Perkins isn't going to get into chicken feed like that. But someone called my dad, said something like your son Raúl won't let us use his posts on the highway there. My dad, and he was fuming, too, asked just who the hell was on the line. Some name. Raza, too. And the guy was hiding behind Perkins's name, using it.

My dad's fuse was shorter than a midget's pencil, know what I mean? Anyway, my dad swore that the guy on the line was a Texas Mexican, and he told him, nicely, too, since he recognized that the guy was just doing his job, earning his pay, but that it would be best to call Ira and have Ira call don Diego Santoscoy. Well, Ira was new in town, and he wouldn't know my dad from a pile of books, and he never did call. Well, after that, I didn't allow political bills anywhere, and then my dad followed suit. Nothing important, nothing major, but just to show you how some people are.

After he got into office ... tell you when it was, just two weeks after P. Galindo left us. Old P. was here with my dad, had his wife Paulita with him, driving him around, making his goodbyes, he said, and either I or my dad, one, asked him about the new County Commissioner; that's important, since my dad's land is on that precinct. P. Galindo, kindly, too, said he was a nice boy.

And though there didn't seem to be any malice in that dying man's voice, I hope no one ever calls me that, thinks of me in those terms. A nice boy.

But Ira's got friends, a wide circle from what I hear. They're just not our friends. I think it's St. James who asks if you can draw sweet and bitter water from the same place ... That apostle just didn't make it down to the Valley, did he?

Drinks González

Drinks González, baptized Saúl. Sexton.

People such as Becky Escobar, NO! not Escobar, Becky Malacara, belonged to a class and category with old money, but not too old. For instance, I knew don Julio Navarrete, her grandfather. The money is sixty years old, let's say, and then, some sixty years ago, I had convinced myself that social classes were necessary for order and for one's well-being. But that was a long time ago.

But let me tell you this, too. In that give and take we call life, one runs into people who earn all kinds of livings. Business, they call it. Making a living. To earn it, then, one needs the proper touch. You hear this in the Valley all the time, *el tacto*. And know what? Becky Malacara has it, and she uses it by being respectful, but truly respectful. That's important. She has what that husband of hers has, what a man you never knew called Jesús Buenrostro had. The one called El Quieto by his family, although everyone uses that name for him now, and him dead after too brief a life ... One standard. And she's no actress, no put on. Here, let me serve my nephew Henry González, the veteran, as an example.

One fine day, Viola Barragán came by, and Viola is a power, right? And I bet I've got some twenty years on her. Maybe more. Sure. I've known her since she married Dr. Peñalosa, and that was a little before the second World War. At least six hurricanes since then, you know that? Well, she was just a kid then and her folks, the Barragán-Surís, married her off to Peñalosa. She must've been a kid of seventeen at the time ... You're much too young to know of of these affairs and things.

146

Much too young.

The listener lights a cigarette and hands it to Sexton González, who's settled down for talk cum digressions; the best way.

You're much too young to even know of these things, but the Doctor, that's Doctor Peñalosa, and I knew him well, he was from Agualeguas; the Doctor, he died, poisoned to death. Not a suicide, though, but more of an accident. Oh, you can still here some tart tongues running on and on that it was murder. No such thing.

Homicide by poison, but accidental, and done by a pharmacist. An apprentice pharmacist. But he's dead, too. Orfalindo Buitureyra, the King of the Parrandas. It's possible it was murder, the Valley's part of the world, isn't it? You live long enough, and with patience on your side, you'll see a million things. For my money, and that's just a saying, it wasn't murder.

Viola became a widow ... and now? A person of business, a handsome woman who walks and talks like a field general and who dresses in the best from top to bottom. Good for her!

But as I was saying, one Sunday Viola came by some time after High Mass, the last one. I'd finished with the sweeping and wiping of the church and benches. I'd checked the candles, the votaries too, and then polished the altar till I made that white marble shine and sparkle, just like the day they brought it in here all the way from a place really Up North. One of those cold states. So, I was doing what I always do: work.

Finished with that, a glass of wine. After this, a sign of the cross and I went out the side door, lit a cigarette and stood ready for my cup of hot chocolate, when this big old car pulled up. I haven't been able to tell a car or its make since the thirties. But, that car was A CAR AND A HALF. *Un carrazo.*

Air, four doors, dark-colored, and maybe even a television set if there is such a thing now that the Japanese have begun to eat the world feet first ... And there came Viola, a cigarette in hand, and holding a hot cup of coffee for me ... Yeah!

I must stop here to let you know that Viola Barragán has always

treated me with respect. Although just about everyone, and that includes those saints and devils of God, the kids, they all call me Drinks,
Viola has always called me Saúl.

So as not to surprise me, so as to bring me up to date, she told me of
my father's old property. My father don Antonio died in '22, and that
property'd been lost on account of taxes. Well, she just bought it, she
told me. That she wanted to open one of her businesses on that lot, and
that she knew that my nephew Henry González had just retired from
the U.S. Army after some twenty or thirty years in there. You follow?

And that she, Viola, wanted to know if Henry had any plans. Was
he just going to laze around for the rest of his life, playing dominoes
and shootin' pool? Was he going to take a drink every day or was he
planning to take up some job so as not to break the routine. Or what?

Didn't even let me answer. That's her style, though. That she was
thinking of opening up a corner store business, some neighborhood
place. That she needed someone she could trust, rely on. Well, we'd
been at this some 10 or 15 minutes, and me without my hot chocolate,
when I asked her to come into the rectory. She took my coffee and put
it in some tray in that big old hearse of hers.

Viola Barragán is not of our parishioners here at Sacred Heart. Me?
I'm a believer, all right, but I don't stink up the place by going to every
Mass every day. I just go to daily Mass and you'll find me there at five
ayem, seven days a week, 'cause it's my duty and obligation since Mass
is a sacrament. BUT! When it comes to converting folks, I leave that to
other people.

Well, once in the rectory, Viola offered me one of her cigarettes,
and I lit her fresh one and mine. Here, with this Zippo. A present from
Father Ornelas, a Klail City boy.

And there went Viola again: "Someone reliable, Saúl. And I'll see
to Henry's kids' education, if they haven't finished it yet." Like that,
see? Said she remembered Emma Zepulveda, Henry's wife, and that
she always saw her as a woman of sense, and that's why she, Viola, had
come to see me on this.

And this wasn't just talk either. Henry's folks are dead, been dead.
For years. That boy joined the army at fifteen; yes, he did. The Army
people came here, to Pérez's Pool Hall and signed him up at twenty-one
dollars a month with uniforms, room and board for three years, five if he
wanted them. That boy got drunk on all that money and stayed drunk
for two weeks until the U.S. Army sent two soldiers for him. Henry,
he wanted to go, but he had lost the time and the date, and the place.
They, the soldiers, put him on the Missouri Pacific nine-fifteen and from
there to Fort William Barret to start a new life. Loved the Army. Never
ate so much and so well. Came back like a balloon, well, almost, 'cause

the U.S. Army don't like you fat, but he, Henry, said he never met a meal he didn't like. And you know, like he said, years later, too, and he wasn't a kid then, a prisoner in Korea, the war many of the boys were in, a prisoner, and he ate everything. Lost weight, but he wasn't skin and bone. He was one of those big sergeants. You can't get no more stripes on him, see? Fills up the sleeves, both of 'em. That's my nephew Henry.

But like I said, Viola wasn't just talking. I told her Henry was ready to work, anytime. And he was. Well, not six months later, that corner store grows out of the ground there, and it's open for business. And there they were, Henry and Emma running the place ... Becky, she runs those stores, and now Henry and Emma own part of it. Becky worked it out this way.

Henry, he was a baker in the U.S. Army, and Becky says why doesn't he open up a bakery on the same lot. Emma runs the store, Henry runs the bakery, and the bakery is theirs. Just like that. Becky says the store will make business because people will come in for both on the way home. That girl was right. And Henry's no drinker, by the way. Ever since he went on that *parranda* on the Army money, he swore never again. Not even a beer.

So, Becky runs the Shopping Bags and that agency of small cafes, the hamburger places. Busy Bees? The Busy Bees, right?

We're not a rich parish, not like others I could name ... but Father Ornelas—he's not the pastor, that's Father Eloy—but Father Ornelas— and I always call him that even if I had known his folks before they even married—anyway, Father Ornelas talks to both Jehu and Becky; and let me tell you, she's business and at the same time, nice. But nice. And with Mexican courtesy for all. There are some people who wouldn't know courtesy if it hit 'em in the face like a water-filled balloon. Anyway, Father Ornelas talks to them. They bring the kids here, to this church, this parish, and they don't live here, in this area. But Jehu grew up with Father Ornelas, see? Now, this is a secret, and I don't have to explain to you what that means. Becky says that Jehu would like to be told if Father Ornelas is ... is threatened with a transfer. Yes.

Old Juvencio Ornelas the Candyman died as a result of the many sugars in his body, and now it's only Petronila Ornelas, and she lives with some old folks. Folks like me, but folks who need more help. Me? I can work. I'm like that man who used to bury people, he now works at the big Bank, *el banco del rancho* ...

Well, Jehu and Becky keep up with people like that. Jehu knew and knows and remembers what being poor means ... Becky? She had money from that old grandfather of hers and from her own father too. But she says that doesn't matter. What matters, and here she sounds a lot like Viola, what matters is what you do. What you do ... I am me, I told her. I explained it in Spanish. *Yo soy yo.*

And now? Everytime she sees me, she says, *"Yo soy yo, don Saúl. ¿Y usted?"* I tell her who I am, *quién soy yo* ... Ha!

Esa Becky is independent, and married too. Reminds me of the late Enriqueta Farías. An old woman when I knew her, and that means going back in God's time. She was Jehu Malacara's great-aunt. Well, Rafe Buenrostro's too, of course. A Relámpago woman. Born there, died there. Religious, but fierce, too. Generous. Lived to be a hundred, maybe more. They live long in that family, unless God calls them early or some man decides ...

As for Becky, well, I've known the Navarretes since 1893, '94. And I let her know who she is, where she comes from ... she likes to know things like that. Respects the past but won't live in it.

Me? Married the once and that was it. Hmmm. St. Paul says it's better to marry than to burn. What did he know? He ever marry? Always traveling, giving advice in that hysterical voice of his. But Dr. Luke? Ah. Remember the crumbs which fell from the rich man's table? It's what you do with them, as Father Ornelas says. And Jehu doesn't hand out crumbs. Money and jobs are far from crumbs ...

Can't say much about Becky's first husband. I never met the City Councilman. Belonged to one of the other parishes. Yes.

Ira Escobar

Now, how could she have come up with such ideas, I ask you. To throw me out of the house. Me! Sounds incredible, doesn't it? My God, who would've thought she'd do something like that?

I park the car, come into the house after a hard day's work with the County Commissioners' Court, and that was it, picked up and dumped like an old dish rag, right to the trash barrel. Just like that.

I asked her three times, four, maybe more, and the answer was the same in each case: "I've decided etcetera, etcetera, etcetera." And I couldn't get her to say anything else. Like a cracked record, "I've decided ... "

The bitch had been changing all along, sure she was, and I bet she didn't even know that I was noticing something new about her. Han! To throw me out of the house; and out of the bed, too. But that was our secret. And the kids? What could they have been thinking about my sleeping in the spare bedroom?

The bitch planned it real good, too. Oh, yeah ... here comes that jackass and there we were, in the living room. The kids by her side. She planned it right down to the last detail. And then? To choose Romeo Hinojosa to represent her? No, whatever anybody says, choosing him was no accident.

God ... everytime something happens on the County level, there he is. Jesus. Aren't there any other lawyers in town? Han! All I can say about him is that he's got nothing else to do but get in the County's hair. Buttinksy! Know-it-all! And nosey? All those rolled up in one ... And let's see? Why isn't he rich if he's such a hotshot? Why, he hasn't got a pot to put a flower in ...

Someone, somewhere, helped him in our divorce every step of the way. What does he know about the law? Someone helped him out, had to. I know I've asked Polín Tapia a thousand times, but even he hasn't been able to find out anything ... Han!

But she sure showed a lack of consideration, and of shame, too. Imagine getting married just eighteen months later? What was the bitch's rush, anyway? Jehu Malacara! You'd swear she'd done it on purpose, to make me look the fool ... Well, all I can say is she's going to learn, and see and know, that Jehu Malacara isn't the bargain she thought he was when they married.

But Jehu too didn't exactly strike oil there; I look upon that marriage as a case of private punishment for Jehu. He'll learn. He'll see just what size pants she wears. Oh, yeah. He who is so sure of himself. He who walks around as if he were bullet-proof or something. He'll see.

And that ought to teach him. Her, too. That Jehu is a regular hell on wheels, and my wi ... well, all I can say is that she better watch out. And I'll say this too: They deserve each other. Yessir.

And will you look at them? That's a lovely role they're acting out, isn't it? As if they were worthy of respect. Han! Why, she's a divorced woman, what my mother calls a woman of the world. A divorced woman turned around and married a Mr. Nothing. A relative of the Buenrostros. Who says so? And what do I care if he is or not? My uncle don Javier said that the Buenrostros, all of them and their relatives, too, that the Buenrostros were, are, and will continue to be a big bunch of hypocrites. That's right! Did you know that the Buenrostros own 200 hectares in Soliseño? Part of the Llano Grande grant? Rafe owns and farms that in Mexico! Right across from the El Carmen Ranch. Is that legal? Probably bribed Mexican officials to farm there!

Yessir. The Buenrostros are not a band of angels. You mean that just because the oldest brother and Rafael were in the service that gives 'em a special place somewhere? I didn't go to Korea 'cause I took and passed a deferment exam when I was up at St. Mary's. And Jehu? What did he do in the Army? Yeah. He himself says he worked as a chaplain's assistant; as if chaplains were in any sort of danger. Han!

But the marriage won't last. How can it? And, neither one knows how to spend money; they lack the talent. Worse, they can't even satisfy the kids when it comes to buying presents, as I can ... and do. But Becky'll see for herself, she'll see what kind of person Jehu is. Yessir.

To begin with, he's not generous, he is one of the most conservative bankers there is and so much so, there's a smell of tight-waddishness there.

It's funny. And her? Becky? Does she think that just because she works with Viola—and how much can she earn, anyway?—does she think she can buy all the clothes she wants? She's the world's leading spendthrift. And him? Why, that man is the orignal Mr. Skinflint, I've never seen a man so tightfisted, and he uses all four fingers and a thumb, too. He thinks he'll keep her happy being the way he is and just because, right? Han!

They'll see, they'll see ...

And Becky too will learn something else, if she hasn't already. Let me ask you this: How many friends does she have? The very few Anglos she knew at the Music Club moved away from Klail City, yeah. And those who stayed, and I can bet you on this, they probably don't even know or care if she's alive. That's right, let me remind you she's no longer The Commissioner's Wife. She's never had less friends than now.

And that's it; goodbye to whatever social life she had, and forever, too, because Jehu lacks the grace and savvy as to how to make new friends. If Becky isn't careful, the bitch'll be like a cloistered nun because that guy is a stay-at-home. For days, weeks even. He's like a hermit, you know. But Becky will see just what kind of trouble she bought when she married Mr. Jehu Malacara. Han!

And that town! Nothing like Jonesville. Everywhere you turn around, so and so is related to so and so, and it doesn't matter if you're first, second or third cousins. They'll fit you in. Why, talk about inferiority complexes where they have to hide behind relatives and such ...

And what does she know about sacrifices? I'm the one who told, pointed out to Noddy Perkins, when that job opened up in Jonesville.

The job at the Klail Bank was taking too much time from County business. And now that I'm here at the Jonesville Savings and Loan, I'm better off by two hundred per cent. Jonesville is a bigger town; it's a city, really. And Noddy's very happy with my performance and my work both here at the S. and L. and in the County.

One has to live one's life, right? There's no reason why I should give up my freedom, is there? My Mom and I have talked on this a thousand times, and we see eye to eye on this.

And look, when Jehu brings the kids to my mother-in-law's, I say it isn't necessary that he wait in the car until he sees them walking through the door. I've told Charlie and Sarah to tell him how I feel about that, but you think he cares? It's not that important, I know, but it's like throwing dirt in my face that he's the one who brings the kids here.

It's a good thing the kids are sweet kids; otherwise they would've insulted Jehu by now. But they weren't raised that way. They should treat everyone with the same respect. This house was established with social responsibilities; it's our form and function.

But those two don't have to worry about me. She's the one who wanted the divorce, and now she's stuck with it. She's the one who wanted to marry Jehu Malacara, and that was a door she opened for and by herself, yessir. She made the decision, well, she's got to hold on to it now, and may God and His Holy Church forgive me, but I wouldn't go back to her even for the kids' sake.

This is not overweening pride; not at all. I look at it as a great favor that's been given me, a boon, something for which I'll be forever grateful when I was rid of her.

No, I'm not coming back for seconds, thank you, no. Here I am, closing in on forty, and I sure won't be the one who's going to cry for someone who doesn't deserve crying for. Oh, no! And doña Elvira better not even think of coming to this house. My mother has never cared for her. In her life. Never.

But there's no danger from that front and so, why worry? I'm the happiest I've ever been, and I, for one, certainly don't wish them any ill-fortune of any kind. And why would I, anyway? What would be the use? Me? I'm content enough to say that they deserve each other, one and the other, and that's nothing less than the Truth itself.

But that's up to them, that life of theirs. They're each going to have a handful putting up with one another. And that's as sure as rain falls somewhere every day, just like it's falling out in Gulf right now. And they're just like the rain, inconsistent.

And you know what she said? What she had the nerve to say? I heard she was talking to Sammie Jo or to Viola, to somebody, anybody who'd listen to her most likely ... Someone had asked her why, why the divorce? Know what the little bitch said? Han! Listen to this and tell me if she isn't going out of her head: "I saved myself. That's all that happened between Ira and me. I saved myself, and I'll let it go at that."

The listener, too, will let it go at that.

Becky

Becky. The listener has nothing to add here. Nor does the listener intend to add a colophone, a coda. Becky, and it's high time, too, should speak for herself.

Years ago, Daddy decided to Mexicanize himself, and so much so that he's not an Anglo anymore, a *bolillo* as Jehu says.

As a kid, when I was with the Scholastics and later on at St. Ann's, we used English and nothing but . . . I spoke English to Mama, and she'd answer me in Spanish. That's pretty normal for Valley mexicanos. Besides, Mama prefers Spanish, and that's it.

Daddy is the sweetest, dearest thing there is. He's a good man in the good sense of the word. Oh, I know what people say, and I've heard it all my life: "All he does is hunt and fish." That's just talk. And Mama? She adores him, and I do too. He is something that people wish they were: kind, giving, and—a word not much in currency—virtuous.

People. People say Mama pushed me into marrying Ira. That's partly true, but I'm the one who made that mistake. I thought I loved Ira, convinced myself I did, and for a long time, too.

And what's the big to-do? Is there a mother who doesn't want her daughter well off? Comfortable? But it happens that I let myself, had placed myself there. I wanted to marry Ira. That I don't love him as a husband now, or that I don't want him to live with me and the kids, that is something I decided as well. I made a mistake a long time ago, and it was up to me to correct it.

Can't I be allowed to make a decision? Must I always accomodate myself, every time?

155

And I certainly didn't talk the divorce over with Mama and Dad beforehand. The difficulty, but difficult only in broaching the subject, was in talking to the kids. Sarah was eight at the time, and Charlie going on eleven. They love their Father, as they should. I insist on it. But they can also see that this is another life, that their Mom has remarried. That Mom works, and that there's nothing wrong in it. As far as I know, the kids have not had the divorce thrown in their faces. If someone were to, old or young, the kids know what to say to that. Now then, that Jehu and I married a year and a half after the divorce is as much our business as it is Charlie's and Sarah's, but no one else's.

Jehu prefers straight talk. I do too, although I had to learn that for myself. It was hard going, but that wasn't Jehu's fault.

And this is what people must understand: Jehu is not the kids' Father; he's their Dad. There shouldn't be any mistake on that score, I don't think. They both love and respect Jehu, and he loves them. When they're not with me or when I can't take them to work with me, Jehu leaves the bank, takes them to the park, to Mom's house, or to see Rafe or Rafe's nephews out at the farm.

The first visits to Mom's house were strained. And why shouldn't they have been? But Time's a great leveler; it's like money, says Jehu. And he laughs when he says it; I do too. And in time, Mom's learned to come around. Mama is a snob, but is that a high crime? Aren't there worse things?

It seems almost a hundred years ago that Ira and I moved to Klail. And then, straight away, Noddy decided that Ira was to run for the Commissioner's post . . . even before we left Jonesville for Klail. Many things happened back then. Personal things.

Among them, I lied for Jehu. I lied to Mr. Galindo. To Noddy. To myself. But I didn't know Jehu then, and I had no way of knowing that Jehu was, is, capable of defending himself, from any quarter. But I lied because I already loved him, and so I sought to protect him from Ira, from Noddy. *That's* funny.

Ollie San Esteban. I do not, nor will I ever, speak ill of Ollie San Esteban or her memory. Never. I was a spoiled, silly, nattering little fool, but with all of that, I sensed somehow that changes had to be made. I knew I wanted Jehu. That's a difference. And we made love; he wanted to, and I wanted to. I wanted to see him, be with him, hold him. I was indiscreet, of course, but I wasn't a fool. All he saw in me was a pretty face. I knew that. But he had to know who I was, what I was.

As for those changes, I didn't have the nerve, the courage, or even the imagination to figure them out. But I learned. Now, alone or with Jehu, here, in our home, I think about what held me back from seeing the changes. It was fear. Finally, one day, I asked myself what it was I feared. The answers came tumbling out, hundreds of them. But then, at that time, I hadn't learned about ultimate questions ... oh, yes. When I asked myself the ultimate question, and I answered yes to myself, and I knew I was dead serious, fear, or whatever it was, flew out that front door, through the porch, and away from this house ...

That day, the kids came in from school, and I prepared some limeade for the three of us. Sarah brought the cookies, I remember, and Charlie set the table ... He was about to go upstairs for his shorts and sneakers, ready to go out and play, but I asked them to sit. For a talk. I had no idea what they'd say, how long I would talk, but talk I did and all of us cried, too. And then we waited for Ira ...

I sat there, I thought I'd done a selfish thing, that I was the same old Becky. And I cried. Just then, Sarah moved over and told me not to cry. And she was just eight-years-old, you understand. Charlie then ran upstairs and put on some long pants and a shirt. We waited. The car, the door, the front porch ...

We were a long way from the first day we'd moved to Klail ... I cut a ridiculous figure. And for a while there, I even pretended to myself that I wasn't Elvira Navarrete's daughter, as if Ira's mother had raised me. Denial, of course; nothing else but.

I had made myself into another person, and, too, I was such a fool I couldn't see Sammie Jo's friendship when it was offered.

And Sammie Jo and I are friends. She's something. *Es persona*. And that is how she saw me. As a person, but I couldn't see myself.

But getting back to Jehu. I was just one more conquest, but hardly that, since there'd been no resistance on my part. I went to him, even when I knew he loved Ollie San Esteban. And why shouldn't he love her, and yes, I also knew about him and Sammie Jo ... And well, was I any better?

But I didn't love Ira. And there were the kids. And people. And Mom ... And then the ultimate question ... what would I do for Jehu to know me so that he would then love me. And so I told Ira that I'd decided he was not to live with us anymore.

That man Jehu ... He called on the San Esteban family for over a year after Ollie's death. A man of responsibilities, you see. And then, twelve months to the very day of the decision, on a day like today, a bit gray and overcast, somewhat windy, hurricane weather, he showed up. There, on the porch.

We sat, and I couldn't stop talking. Poor Jehu. But I didn't care
what he thought of me then and there. What I wanted to know, all I
wanted to know, was did he love me, did he love me as I loved him? But
thank God Jehu is the way he is. He nodded and looked at me for the
longest time. I couldn't know, of course, but I felt it.

I don't know about you, but have you ever had someone look at you,
up close, eye to eye? A clear, unclouded, an almost unblinking look at
you? Jehu looked at me that way that afternoon.

I didn't ask him to say he loved me, I wasn't a kid. But he said it
anyhow. One surprise after another, that man.

And then? He said to call the kids, to go out, for a walk, on the
sidewalk, around the block. And Sarah, who'd never seen him, took
his hand, hugged him. Sarah! Yes. And kissed him. Even the weather
helped; the wind calmed down, as calm as the kids.

Charlie? Charlie ran up to his room and brought back a sketch he'd
drawn at the Scholastics. When Jehu smiled, Charlie gave it to him: a
present. I don't think they said a word between them.

Since much Spanish common property law prevails in Texas, the
management and apportionment of property took time. It was Jehu
who suggested that Romeo Hinojosa represent me. Jehu then said it
would be better if he didn't call on me until after the divorce. He then
explained this to the kids: clearly, simply, no embellishment. Well, Mr.
Hinojosa made an excellent case for me and the kids, although I must
say that Ira behaved like a pig in this. Kept bringing up the fact, his
lawyer did, that Jehu had called on me. Poor Ira! He still doesn't understand a thing.

That's been two years now, and the trouble with Ira is that he can't
see beyond tomorrow. The kids are growing up, and they may wind up
not loving Ira because of Ira's behavior. Jehu, now, he will not allow
the baby, Sarah, or Charlie either, for that matter, he won't allow them
to speak disrespectfully about Ira. Jehu says that isn't done. He, too,
never says a word against Ira, and so, the kids follow his example: no
criticism.

Don't mistake what I say, though. Jehu knows Ira for the fool he is.
And he knows that Noddy controls Ira, who doesn't know the first word
about banking or little else. Jehu says Noddy knows this, and since Ira
likes the easy way out of things, Noddy keeps him under wraps.

As for Noddy, he can throw both Jehu and Ira out of the banking
business and into the streets any time he wants to. It's his bank. But
Jehu doesn't care, and poor Ira does care. That's the difference.

And this is my new life, and it's the best one I could have chosen.
There's no set routine to our lives... As I said earlier, Jehu comes home
at noon, on a Wednesday, say, he'll call the bank and say he won't be

back that afternoon. He'll drive to Klail Mid-School, sign out for the kids, and if I've got nothing pressing at the moment, we'll drive out to El Carmen Ranch and visit a while.

That's Jehu, impromptu. It's the same with the few parties we give at home. A few people we know, mostly family.

For Jehu it's always the family. Me. The children, that's the first family. And then the other family, Rafe, who's more than just a cousin. They're like kids, they call each other on the phone.

And speaking of Rafe, Jehu wanted to postpone the wedding, and I was for it. Rafe was recuperating from his eye trouble again, but Rafe wouldn't hear of it. Got me on the phone, "*No lo dejes*," is what he said.

People who don't know Rafe think he's reserved; that's the word I always hear. He's quiet, sure, and he's certainly that way in public. He's funny, though. Like Jehu, he laughs, he can tell a joke ...

To me, Jehu is the reserved one. And patient? I think that's why the kids also love him. He's incredibly patient ... and you know, it takes a good business head and sense to be patient. I learned that on my own.

I won't talk about my work or what I do at Barragán Enterprises. It's boring to talk about it, but it's something else to live it. It's my professional life; that's all there is to that.

Viola? I was wrong about her as I was wrong about many things. She loves me as if I were her own daughter, had she had one ... I learned the business by watching her, by being there ... and I remember my first important lesson in business: *Yes* means *yes*, and *no* means *no*. Negotiations are always preliminaries, but the yeas and nays are the finalities ...

I talked to few people about what I wanted to do ... I talked to Mrs. Campoy, a hundred if she's a year, and bright and lucid ... I also talked to Viola. Before I talked to Mama. See? And Viola? She cried. But do you see? We're talking about a fearless woman here. And she was the first to see what was in me, before I could even see for myself. Saw it before Jehu, too.

And that's it. I'm not a woman who was saved, redeemed. I saved myself. With help, of course. With love and good will, too, and all the rest. But if I couldn't save myself, if I couldn't save me from myself ... But why go on?

Let's say I saved myself, and let it go at that.

Yes, the listener will also let it go at that.

End Note

... what a strange accident the truth is.

George Santayana